Remington and the Mysterious Fedora

www.writebyme.ca

ISBN: 1-4609-5140-9
ISBN-13: 9781460951408

Remington and the Mysterious Fedora

A novel by

Chuck Waldron

2011

Dedication

None of this would be complete without recognizing the people who have helped my stay the course. First, my special thanks to Suzanne, my wife of over 43 years. When I wanted to quit, her encouragement and belief in my writing kept me going.

When I needed the competent touch of an editor, it was my good fortune to meet Darcie. Her professional editing and suggestions helped me create a book I could be proud of.

Thanks to all the others who offered support and encouragement. You know who you are.

To Beehey 2012
Mt. Dora Chuckles

Also By Chuck Waldron

Tears in the Dust
Served Cold

"Would I have phrases that are not known, utterances that are strange, in new language that has not been used, free from repetition, not an utterance which has grown stale, which men of old have spoken?"
Author unknown

He braked and locked his bike to a nearby fence railing. Walking through the door, he took a moment to let his eyes adjust to the lighting inside store. He became aware of an odor, the whiff of what? *Stuffy,* he decided.

They could use some lights. Even I'm not this cheap.

Inside the door on his right was a display counter. It reminded Josh of a photo he had seen once, a photo of a dry goods store in some rural town in the early twentieth century. The date on the photo was 1911, he recalled after a minute's thought.

A man of indeterminate age stood behind the counter in the dusty store. Josh never saw a banker's eyeshade before. (He learned later such visors were worn by all sorts of people, bankers, clerks and gamblers.) The man behind the counter had one; it was green. Josh saw the man's eyes peering out from under the visor, but there was no way he could guess the nature of the man looking at him.

The clerk didn't say anything, merely pulled a worn cardigan together at the front and stared at him. Josh waited, but the man didn't say anything.

Deciding to break the ice, Josh said, "I've never seen your store before. Did you just open it? Where did you get all this incredible old stuff?" Josh waved his arm around at all the miscellaneous mish-mash surrounding him. He thought he detected a faint smile emerge from under the visor.

"New or old, merely words," the man said.

What is this guy talking about? Josh said to himself, not given to scatological language, even in his thoughts. The truth was, Josh was growing more than a bit nervous, and as he was deciding to leave, the man said, "Why not take your time and look around. You never know what treasures you might find."

Josh turned back around. "Is there any organization to things here?"

"Just start looking," the man said with a shrug. "Isn't the best part of a journey the journey itself? Look, discover, take pleasure in the search itself." The man waved to one side, "There are two more rooms. This room I call old, the second room I call older, and you can guess what I have in the last room," he finished and started a phlegmatic coughing, not bothering to cover his mouth.

Josh didn't like the sound of the cough, but he was intrigued. He started to ask another question, but the man turned to pick up a book. He began reading intently, oblivious to the young man on the other side of the counter. For no apparent reason, Josh noted the man was reading *Moby Dick.*

Josh didn't find anything of interest in the first room. He kept looking back over his shoulder, but the store owner was paying no attention to him now. There was a pile of old magazines that caught Josh's attention: *Life, Look, National Geographic,* and something called *The Fiddlehead,* which turned out to be a Canadian literary magazine from 1945.

He moved on, fingering some glassware, but nothing on those shelves grabbed his attention. He pushed his plastic glass frames up a little further on his nose and stifled a sneeze, tickled to life from the dust.

He found the second room even more interesting. In the corner of the room he spotted some racks of vintage clothing. Alongside was a shelf of old headwear. He was intrigued with a particular tall hat. He picked it up and held it, eyes wide with curiosity, turning it in his hand. He looked at the headband on the inside, looking for a clue that would tell him what kind of hat it was.

"They called it a stove-pipe hat, back in the day. I always wondered if that hat you're holding might've belonged to Abraham Lincoln himself," the shop owner said with a chuckle. He crept into the room to stand behind Josh, and started to cough again. It was an unpleasant cough, really, the man reaching for a handkerchief this time and holding it to his lips. "Try it on.

There's a mirror in here someplace." The man shuffled off into another room, and Josh put the hat back on the shelf.

He placed it next to another interesting looking hat. It was camel-colored, with a dark brown ribbon wrapped around it, just above the brim, a fedora. Josh picked it up and tried it on. He finally located the mirror and almost started to laugh.

I look just like Indiana Jones.

If older, he might have said *Gene Kelley* or *Humphrey Bogart*. If only slightly older, he might have conjured up images of Freddy Kruger or one of the Blues Brothers. But Josh was in his middling years and Indiana Jones was within his range of understanding.

He put the hat back on the shelf, unaware of any provenance or magical qualities. But as he drew his hand back, he was surprised that his fingers felt quite tingly from touching the hat. He felt something else when he was wearing the hat. It made him feel almost...dizzy. No, that wasn't quite it. It felt like something was putting thoughts into his head, thoughts he couldn't quite identify. The feeling slowly dissipated as he put the hat back on the shelf. Josh moved on into the third room, ignoring the hat.

He looked around the room and saw an amazing collection. It wasn't just old, it was *old*. There was a thick layer of dust covering everything, which belied the idea that this was a newly-opened establishment.

It was a mismatched collection of furniture and equipment and other odds and ends. Nothing particularly attracted Josh's attention, and he randomly picked up boxes to open, only to close and return them to their places.

He was almost ready to leave, his thoughts having drifted back to the hats. He wanted to look at them one last time before he left. As he turned to retrace his steps back to the second room, he noticed an old wooden pallet leaning up against the back wall. He saw something behind it, something black and metallic. Curiosity more than anything caused him to pull back the pallet, until he saw a heavy-looking *something* sitting on the floor. Josh didn't recognize it and didn't have a clue it was a key to his future.

What he saw was a squarish lump of metal with a keyboard. He didn't identify it at first, and if it hadn't been for a photo he saw once, a picture of Ernest Hemingway's study, would never have guessed that it was a typewriter.

Intrigued, he pulled the pallet away and leaned it back against the wall to the left. The typewriter sat there, lonely and expectant.

Josh knelt down and touched the cold, black metal, brushing away the thick layer of dust that covered it like matted dryer lint. Just above the tiers of keys he could make out a name. He brushed more dirt away, licking his thumb and rubbing until he could read it: *Remington*. There was a metal frame wrapped around in front of the keyboard. He could see each key—round, with worn silver letters in the center. Each key was circled by a silver metal band and the letters were each filigreed in the same silver metal against a jet black background. He pushed down on one and heard a click as the key pushed an arm up inside the case. Each key was connected to a slender arm with a tiny metal plate at the end that extended from the interior of the typewriter.

It was a manual typewriter, not even an electric cord to plug into the nearest outlet. He suddenly realized he was looking at the ancestor of his computer keyboard. A sense of awe and reverence washed over him.

He picked it up and was surprised at the weight. This was some heavy piece of office equipment.

"Do you know what you are holding?" Josh almost dropped the typewriter at the voice sounding from behind. He turned to the old man while managing to pull the beast closer to his chest for safe keeping.

"I know it's a typewriter, I've seen pictures and read about them, but..."

"It still works," the man said, "or at least, it did when I bought it. More like a gift it was. Almost free, it was." The man started coughing again. "I asked the lady how much she wanted for it. I got it for five bucks. Imagine a classic typewriter like that for five dollars!"

As Josh turned it in his arms, the carriage slipped to the side, creating imbalance, and a bell rang. He almost dropped it again, unsure.

The old man chuckled. "That bell rings when the carriage gets to the end. That's how the secretaries knew to push this." He stepped closer and pointed to a silver metal arm on the right that extended outward and was slightly curved.

"Here, let me take that, young man." He carried it over to the counter and placed in stronger light. Despite his age, the man carried the typewriter as though it weighed no more than a feather.

He showed Josh how the carriage slid back and forth and ran his hand lovingly over a long rubbery cylinder. He brushed the rack, which lay just behind what he called the *platen*, and the name *Remington Rand* stood out. "They did more than make guns, you know." The man laughed and again started that discomforting cough that made Josh nervous.

Josh couldn't believe how much that damn thing weighed. But there was just something about it. *What is it? What is speaking to me? This machine needs a home.*

For some reason he couldn't explain, he turned to the clerk, who he now thought looked quite ancient. *Why didn't I noticed his age before?*

"How much?"

"Like I said, it cost me five dollars. I have always thought it fair to make a profit, but I have never embraced greed. Hmmm...let me see...twenty, no, twenty five percent." Josh watched the old man's fingers pushing an imaginary calculator in the air and finally said, "I need a twenty-five percent mark-up. Yep, that'll make the price to you at $5.75."

"You *are* kidding, right?"

"Not for you," the man said, his eyes narrowing slightly as he stared Josh in the eye.

Unnerved a bit, Josh fished money out of his pocket. Paper money and coins were all jammed together in a twisted crumple. He offered the man more, but the old man looked offended. "I know what I'm doing, young man," was all he said.

Josh carried the typewriter out to his bicycle and was faced with the task of carrying it while balancing unsteadily on the bike. He finally decided to heft it under his right arm and started to pedal. He swerved a bit and finally figured out his balancing act. He was almost a block away when something made him stop.

That hat...the fedora!

He stopped, almost dropping the Remington again. He dropped the bike against a retaining wall and didn't bother to lock it. He ran at a walk, back to the store with the typewriter under his arm. He placed it on the counter and walked straight back to the second room. The hat was still there, that camel-colored fedora with the dark brown ribbon wrapped around, just above the brim. He placed it on his head. The old man was waiting.

"How much?" Josh asked.

"What's the sign on this store," the old man laughed. "Cheap Stuff, eh?"

Josh waited.

Again the old man said, "Hmmm..." and started some internal calculations. This time Josh knew to wait quietly.

"Two ought to do. Yep, two bucks."

Josh made quite an impression riding down the street—an old Remington typewriter under his arm and a tan fedora rakishly tilted on his head. His bike weaved from side to side, and ignored the occasional honking of impatient motorists passing him by.

"Kelsey!" he yelled when he got back to the apartment. "You are not going to freakin' believe this!" He dropped the typewriter with a loud *kerthunk!* Kit sat on top of what passed for their coffee table.

"What the hell is that?" Her mouth hung open in question as she walked down the hall toward him. "You do bring the damndest-"

"I have to go back down and get my bike. Wait," he held up his hand.

"And what is *that* on your head?" she laughed.

He ran out the door, and when he finally returned with his bike, he was out of breath.

"There I was, riding along minding my own business, when I saw this store. Strange, Kelsey, I ride by there all the time. I've never noticed it before. Anyway, there I was when I went in it was just *amazing*."

Kelsey was used to his rambling and waited for him to tell her.

"This old man—what a character, let me tell you—had all this stuff. Most of it was junk, but look at that—an old typewriter. He said it works. It's crazy, but I just *had* to have it for some reason.

"It doesn't look like it works to me," Kelsey said. "And what about that filthy hat you're wearing? Yuck!"

He tried to put it on her head, but she shook her red hair and slapped it away with her left hand. "You're not putting that thing on *my* head!"

chapter

THREE

Let me introduce you to Joshua Cody, born in 1988. With energy to burn, he is bright, but has a tendency to take on more challenges than time allows. What does he have to prove? For one, that he is better than tall people, a compensation for feeling short, being just 5-foot 3-inches tall.

To make matters worse for Joshua, his latest girl friend is a towering 5'9" tall, a spectacular beauty, and the most popular girl on campus. Her name, you ask? Why, Kelsey, of course.

Josh is, to put a fine point to it, the consummate nerd. He keeps pushing thick-lens glasses back up on his nose, a habit that annoys others around him. Of course, he chose the bulky, black frames himself and considered they were quite the thing, being cheap and all. The only thing missing from his portrait as a consummate nerd was a pocket protector, and he would have looked right at home on a 1958 campus in Nowhere, Iowa.

He's not good looking, with a personality to match. That is to say, unpleasant. Having said that, you are naturally going to ask me why Kelsey would hang around someone like Josh, let alone be considered his "girl."

Josh may be a nerd, lacking completely in personality, and might go totally unnoticed in a crowd, except for one thing: His intelligence was totally off the charts. Josh is a damned genius.

His singular problem was in finding an outlet for all the things bouncing around in his extra big brain. One moment you would be listening to him expound on the effects of global warming on the fishing inventory off the Grand Banks. Seconds later, he would do a 180 and start citing the statistics of an obscure baseball game from 1971, long before his birth. While he was doing that, he was always doodling: a diagram on a scrap piece of paper or bit of napkin, a mathematical formula analyzing geographic economics, scrawled on the cover of a *Playboy* lying on the coffee table...

And it should come as no surprise to anyone that he fancied himself a writer—a writer who just accepted a challenge to write a novel in less than a month.

He discovered a website one day while he was working on a graphic design for a project. It described a challenge to write a 50,000-word novel in a month. Like I said, Josh has a problem with focus and multi-tasking.

Josh acknowledged his latest goal of writing a novel in a month *might* take some concentration. He knew he needed to avoid the usual distractions that sent electrical impulses flashing around his brain.

He looked at the clock, 4:30 a.m., and the residue of the latest cup of coffee was off to the side. It had developed an unwelcome color and was beyond tepid; in fact, it was quite cold. He was not one to stand in line to order a latte at a popular corner coffee shop. In a departure from his usual approach to brewing coffee, he scooped crystals of instant coffee into a cup and filled it with hot water from the tap. Fast was more important than taste or cheap; he was in a hurry. The cleanliness of the cup was not a concern, either. Kelsey often turned away in revulsion when she saw the cups he was willing to use, often sitting on the counter all night with some unknown liquid leaving a ring around the cup when he dumped out the contents into the sink.

As he sat he felt beads of sweat forming on his forehead and didn't recognize the signs of over-caffeination, combined with anxiety. He tried to ignore the recurring, blinding pain that stabbed the right side of his head from time to time.

"What time is it?" Kelsey appeared in the door. She was wearing a long t-shirt that said "Ennui." It was just long enough to cover any indecency. "Joshua, whatever are you doing?"

Josh heard the question and it felt like his head was going to explode. Instead of answering, he closed his eyes and remained silent.

Shoeless, he stretched his feet out and noticed a hole in the toe of his left sock. He ignored Kelsey, the coffee cup, the slight electronic odor of his laptop, and allowed himself to be drawn to an imaginary place.

He pictured himself alone in a darkened theater, looking up at a blank white screen, and willed his body to relax, each muscle group finding a place of comfort inside his body. As his mind settled on that place envisioned on the screen, he imagined watching the scene unfold. He knew it was a technique, and he knew he wasn't really watching a screen in a theater, but he felt all the tension slipping away, regardless.

He opened his eyes and turned to Kelsey, "I think I would rather be sailing."

Thus began a story within this story. A writer planning his next novel, a young man who can't quite focus his own writing voice, waking up from an imagined scene, he can only remember parts, like shards of a broken vase recovered from an archeological dig.

He starts with a part he can remember, the story of a young girl lying on pebble rocks in a cold, fast-rushing stream. He uses those shards to piece together the thread of a novel.

He has no idea where the thought are coming from. Joshua Cody is a strange young man indeed.

chapter

FOUR

Josh was puzzled by Kelsey's reaction to the typewriter and hat. He thought they were so obviously cool, and it was clear she *didn't*. They ate lunch in silence, a sure sign to Josh that she was totally pissed at him, though he wasn't sure why, and didn't want to open the topic up for discussion. He was sure that the reasons for her anger should be apparent to him, and it would only make her more pissed if he admitted he didn't know why.

He learned not to argue with her when she was in that mood. Instead, he got up and cleaned off his plate and glass and walked into the bedroom. He looked around at the disorder, a reflection of his brain in a lot of ways. There was a lot crammed into a small space, but all clearly lacking in organization.

He took off his bike-riding clothes and threw them in a heap in the corner. He stripped off his briefs, preferring Jockeys, looking for racing stripes and pleased to see none.

He scratched his testicles as he walked into the bathroom and turned on the shower. When it was steaming hot, he stepped in and took a long time soaping and rinsing, the whole time pondering his new purchases.

He rubbed down with the towel and felt a slight hint of arousal as he brushed across his prick. He thought about Kelsey for a moment and then remembered her sour mood. *Maybe later would be better*, he thought, ignoring the feeling. *Besides...that typewriter...*

The thought drifted out of his consciousness as he looked around the room for suitable clothes. He finally found a clean pair of khaki cargo pants, which luckily happened to be his favorite. He tucked in his t-shirt—the one with the hammer and sickle—and then pulled it out again, letting it hang nonchalantly past his waistline.

He slipped his feet into a pair of sandals and walked out to the living room. Kelsey managed to look occupied with a book as she sat in a corner chair with her legs curled under her.

Damn, she can look so...

Josh shook his head and turned to the typewriter. He picked it up and carried it out to the kitchen, where he put it on the table under a bright light. He sat and looked at it for a while, unsure of what to do next. He struck some keys and watched as they responded by jumping out of hiding to strike the black, rubbery cylinder.

It was all a mystery to him, watching a mechanical reaction to striking a key. It made so much noise—a clacking sound. It was all very different from the soft ticking of the keyboard on his computer, quiet noises when he tapped the computer keys, the words appearing on the screen. This typewriter was definitely different, he realized.

It was this comparison to his computer that gave him the idea. *Of course—Google it!*

Josh brought his laptop in and opened it next to the typewriter. Seventy years of technology separated his laptop from the ancient typewriter. He waited for the notebook to power up. When his notebook was ready, he typed "Remington" into the search engine box, and within micro seconds, he had several options: razors, guns, beard trimmers, colleges and an odd assortment of things, none of which were associated with typewriters. Frustrated, he added "typewriter" to the search box and was soon on a path to discovery.

One web site directed him to check the serial number and even instructed him on how to locate that number. He turned the typewriter over and saw the darkened little metal plate, stamped with the number *309185S*. He dutifully entered the information into the website serial number box and waited for the page to change. When the site finished processing the information, he saw that he was the proud owner of a Remington 1610M, made between 1936 and 1938. It was the forerunner of the J model built in 1939.

"Kelsey, you have to see this."

She didn't respond and he saw her concentrating even harder on her reading.

Then he saw what he was looking for. A website advertised a service manual for his typewriter. It was available for download and only cost $19.49. It wasn't long until Josh had a service manual on his laptop, complete with photos and diagrams of the parts.

Josh set everything in his life aside for three days and totally immersed himself in his new/old typewriter. He decided to honor it by naming it Remington—Remy for short. He recognized the name was far from creative or original. At the end of the three days, he was familiar with each working part. He found how to open the top, exposing the key connectors underneath. He was able to straighten out two of them that were slightly bent, which caused them to catch on the keys to the side.

He judiciously squirted machinist's oil on each and every moving part, and soon, the keys, the carriage return and the rest of the moving parts were working perfectly.

The service guide provided clear instructions on loading the ribbon. Josh saw how the keys would come up and strike against paper that was wrapped around the platen cylinder. As the keys came up, the ribbon bar would also rise, allowing the keys to strike against the ribbon and press the implant of a letter on the paper.

Most clever, he admitted. *They figured out how to do that without using a software design application.*

I have to add that Josh wasn't really so naïve as it might appear. He did know the evolution of the typewriter and how computer designers knew to use a QWERTY keyboard, making the brave new world easier for people who already knew how to type. Still, he was amazed at the mechanical quality of the machine sitting on the kitchen table.

In the three days he was awash in Remy's history and technical make-up while Kelsey would put her book down and quietly made sure Josh had something to eat and drink. It was his singular brilliance and dedication to learning new things that attracted him to her in the first place.

She knew he had long moved past what pissed her off, conceding to that fact, and in the process, she became quite interested in the metal brute on their table.

"What's wrong?" she asked, seeing his furrowed brow.

He kept peering at Remy and looking at the screen on his notebook computer. "I need a ribbon." For the first time in three days, Josh tore his eyes away from his new friend and actually looked at her.

I didn't expect it to be this hard," he admitted, peering at his computer. "Apparently, they haven't made this kind of ribbon in years. There are collectors and specialty shops that offer ribbons for electric typewriters, but nothing for something like this."

He held up the two spools for her inspection. She took them, turning them around and finally said, "Why not get one of those electric typewriter ribbons," pointing to the computer screen, "and take the ribbon off them and wind them on here." She held the two spools up with a faint smirk. He grinned back.

"Grab your bike and I'll get mine. We can ride to the big box office store and I want to show you the place where I got this."

On their way back home with extra packages of ribbon (just in case), Josh led Kelsey on a mission to find the odd little store where he found the Remington. "It's right around here. Look for the sign," he said, breathing hard as he pedaled, "*Cheap Stuff*—you can't miss it."

They circled the block, circled again, and gradually widened their search.

"Where is this cheap stuff store?" she asked, becoming slightly frustrated by the fruitless circling.

"It was right here, I'm sure."

Josh straddled the bar on his bike, a foot planted firmly on either side. He turned and looked in all directions, forehead crinkled and eyes worried.

"Look—see that railing? The one right there," he said, pointing, "I locked my bike there..." But, there were no junk stores to be found for blocks. No matter how many times Josh looked up and down the street, the store refused to appear.

Then he had an awful thought. *This is all a bizarre dream. I'm going to wake up soon. Stores don't just appear and disappear at random...Do they?*

But, he couldn't acknowledge it as a dream. As he stared at the hardware store in front of him, he heard Kelsey ask in a slightly worried voice, "What's going on, Josh?"

"It's too freakin' insane, that's what's going on. I tell you, Kelsey, this is starting to scare the hell out of me."

chapter

FIVE

While Josh struggled to comprehend the odd little store that appears and disappears on a whim, don't forget about the fedora, the hat that tingled Josh's scalp when he first tried it on.

When he returned to the apartment that fortuitous day of discovery, he was so excited about Remington that he dropped the hat unceremoniously on the radiator. Kelsey didn't even want to touch it, as grimy and distressed as it looked.

The brim was twisted out of shape, and greasy fingerprints were evident. The inside was lined with a leather band. There was the traditional fedora crease down the length of the crown, and someone had exaggerated the pinch in the front of that crease, pinching in on both sides. Kelsey vaguely remembered her grandfather wearing such a hat, but even he switched to wearing the ubiquitous baseball caps later in life. Even though he looked silly doing it, her grandfather turned his ball cap backwards in imitation of kids at the shopping mall.

She tried to make out the label inside the fedora, to see who made the hat. At some level in her mind, she recognized it was unique.

"I think some gangster wore this," Josh laughed.

When she found the nerve to pick it up to check the label, she felt a burning sensation on her fingers. Not burning exactly, but definitely a heat. She quickly dropped the hat back on the radiator in surprise, vowing never to touch it again.

When they got back from the bike ride, Josh was visibly shaken. He couldn't understand why he couldn't find that old store where he bought the typewriter and fedora. "I just don't understand. It's spooky." He couldn't stop talking about it.

Kelsey was surprised. *He must be pretty upset.*

Josh asked for help and between the two of them they managed to transfer the ribbon from a new spool to one of Remington's spools. Josh checked the service manual and carefully installed the spool, running the ribbon to a second, receiving spool. He tightened the tension and looked pleased.

He read the directions and inserted a sheet of paper. Closing the clamp, the paper clung tightly against the platen.

After a moment, he struck a key. For whatever reason, it happened to be the J key. The key connector did the job; the key flew up and struck the ribbon. The ribbon dropped back down and there on the paper, the letter J stood proudly in stark contrast to the white of the page.

"Totally unreal..." he whispered.

Kelsey had to agree.

He sat, his fingers poised over the keyboard. Then he started to type. He wasn't used to the strength it took to push the keys, what it took to move them. But with practice, he soon was typing on the new/old keyboard. He watched the letters appear on the paper: "now is the time for all good men..."

He kept typing until the carriage came to the end and the bell sounded. He reached his left hand up and pushed the carriage back to the right using the silver, curved handle. When he did it the paper advance to the next line and he was ready to type the next letters. Josh smiled with pleasure.

Wow, he said to himself, *it makes a lot of noise, but it actually works!*

He typed some more, and soon was feeling more at ease, but it was slow going. *How did anyone ever pick up any speed on these things?*

He read of secretaries who tested at over 100 words per minute. At the rate he was going, he was far behind that score. He would be lucky if he was pushing 20.

He put another sheet of paper in and, looking at his watch, began to time his typing. At the one-minute mark, he stopped and counted 26 words. And he thought he was going pretty fast.

"Josh, you need to take a break."

He swiped his fingers through his hair. He knew she was right and heard the popcorn kernels snapping open in the microwave. "I know you like the old movies," she said with a tempting smile, "I found this at the library—*Foreign Correspondent.* A reporter in London uncovers a spy ring during World War II." She turned the cover over and read some more. "Alfred Hitchcock directed it. It was made in 1940."

Josh was a history buff and was fascinated by World War II stories. He was also a huge Alfred Hitchcock fan.

"When does the show start?"

They opened a beer each, sat down to a large bowl of buttered popcorn and watched as the DVD player power up. When the menu came up, Kelsey picked the "Play Movie" option, and they watched the movie credits begin to play across the TV screen.

"It's odd, isn't it?" Josh said suddenly. "They put the cast and credits at the beginning in those days. Do we know who Joel McCrea is? I think we've seen him in something before.

Kelsey nodded with a mouthful of popcorn, as she snuggled against Josh's shoulder. The movie started and Josh commented, "I always thought black and white was more dramatic."

They always had these discussions with each old movie, and they couldn't argue because they both agreed.

Josh was watching the movie but feeling slightly distracted. He couldn't take his mind off the Remington. He kept looking back through the kitchen door. The typewriter sat there, waiting for him. Josh turned back to the movie and his jaw dropped.

"Quick, hit pause. Quick, damn it! Stop...now go back. There! Look at the reporter."

They saw the reporter in the moving, hunched over a typewriter, clackity-clacking away at a story. Josh was convinced it was the same model Remington as the one sitting in his kitchen.

"Bitchin'," he said. "And look at what he's wearing. Is that a fedora?"

Kelsey agreed that it was, feeling a little spooked by the coincidence.

"He looks so cool, the cigarette hanging from his lips while he types."

Kelsey looked disapprovingly at the smoking cigarette. "Didn't he know smoking is bad?"

Joshua got up from the sofa and walked over to the radiator and picked up the hat. He looked back at the movie screen frozen on pause. The hat was pushed back on the head of Joel McCrea, black hair just visible under the brim when the camera panned head-on. Josh put his fedora on, imitating the same style.

"Kelsey," was all he was able to say. As he placed the hat on his head, he was overwhelmed by an uncontrollable urge to walk into the kitchen and sit at the typewriter. Like a robot, he reached mechanically for a sheet of paper, inserted it, and started to type. He watched the words appearing on the paper and was completely unaware of where they came from or how they were emerging from the tips of his fingers, not connected at all to any thoughts going through his brain.

Kelsey got up and came to the kitchen with a frown. "I thought we were watching a movie." She stopped abruptly when she saw the look on his face. She bent over and read the paper as he slid the return to begin a new line. "What's that Josh? What does it mean *'Cold Stones in the Water'*?"

"I don't have a clue," Josh said, his fingers continuing to work methodically over the keys.

"It looks like a story. When did you think this up?"

Josh didn't answer. He didn't have an answer. Kelsey eventually backed away and faded into the living room sofa. He kept typing until he was feeling too tired to continue. He stood up to get another beer and took the hat off to wipe his forehead. As soon as he did, the words of the story trapped inside the hat simply broke away from understanding.

What in the world is going on here, Josh wondered. The hair on the back of his head stood on end as he backed away from Remington and the fedora, back pedaling away from the kitchen.

chapter

SIX

Kelsey was far more complicated than people realized. At first glance, she appeared superficial. She was tall, thin, bright red hair, green eyes the color of jade, and of course, freckles to complete the look. Her pepper-sized freckles were overlaid upon a porcelain complexion, without blemish.

In short, she endured envious looks from other women. Of course, "envy" is really a nice way of referring to the green-eyed monster: jealousy. Jealousy and resentment filled the eyes and faces of many who secretly wanted to steal her looks—or at least wished a visitation by a plague of acne on that perfect complexion.

Some young boys learned early on that they could pull up the covers, close their eyes and quickly masturbate to completion with the image of her dancing under their closed eyelids. There were even some young girls who enjoyed the same desires. Her looks were like a magnet that aroused sensual, sexual thoughts. Many—if not most—never looked past that surface to find a lively wit and deep curiosity underneath.

Everyone has at least a few flaws, right? The same was true for Kelsey; as perfect as she looked, she hadn't escaped that natural law. Kelsey's imperfection lie in having a temper that was so volatile, she was often like a seething volcano, ready to erupt. All it took was the wrong word, the wrong look, the wrong body language, and she became a wild mustang with twitching muscles and flaring nostrils, ready to buck and kick at whoever was nearest to her.

Above all the flaws and perfections, however, Kelsey was a very clever young woman. In fact, she was downright intelligent, like a lightening rod to the electricity of someone like Josh.

Josh and Kelsey had been living together for almost a year, and anyone who knew them also knew to stay well away when the two of them were fighting. It was something that occurred frequently, and generally, for the slightest offence either one of them might take. Both were quite sensitive that way.

Tonight was not a night for fighting, however. She recognized to some degree what was happening to Josh, the mesmerized mumbo-jumbo thing with the typewriter. While she did think it was silly of him to give the damn thing a name, *Remy*, she long ago accepted his idiosyncrasies, including that part of him leading to total immersion in a new project. She also knew he could just as quickly lose interest and move on to something entirely new. But, while he was absorbed, his focus was complete. Her temper cooled by the time he came to bed.

Lying beside him that night, she knew he wasn't asleep. She recognized the tossing and turning as he struggled to sort out details in his head, attempting to find order and rearrange facts until he could come to some sort of understanding about whatever problem was troubling him.

She thought it was odd that he could arrive at solutions with the speed of a blink on some occasions, and struggle for hours and days at others. Tonight was one of those times of struggle.

She was annoyed when he turned, pulling the covers away from her with a grunt and a fart, and then finally fell asleep to a gentle snore. Then, as she hovered close to her own sleep, he would come awake again without warning, only to turn the other direction, his knees poking into her from behind. She held her pillow tight to avoid putting it over his face and holding it there.

Instead of smothering him with the pillow, another urge snuck into her consciousness without warning. It came like a thief, a burglar who jimmied a door and was now creeping around in the dark recesses of her mind.

Kelsey was a young woman who was hardwired to sexual pleasure, something she learned to embrace without shame. The digital clock blinked 2:47 when she felt the first wave of arousal wash slowly over her. She never knew when, exactly, something like that started, but she recognized the warmth that was now enveloping her like a toasty blanket.

She snuggled down into the growing tingling sensation and allowed her body to relax, acknowledging each part of her body's contact with the sheets. She rolled her shoulders slightly, pushed down on the small of her back, clenched the cheeks of her buttocks tighter, and felt the heels of her feet touching the coolness of the sheet, a stark contrast to the growing heat she was feeling inside.

Her right hand moved slowly down her stomach until it was poised, ready. Instead, she paused and turned to her semiconscious partner, who was grumbling and muttering with his back to her.

A few minutes later, Kelsey and Josh were spooning on sweaty sheets, blankets kicked off, and the two of them no longer sleepless.

chapter

SEVEN

Josh realized the value of breakfast. He studied nutrition with the same energy he devoted to solving complex mathematical formulas. As a result, he elevated breakfast to the point of worship. It needed to be exact: a balanced meal comprised of whole wheat cereal in just the right amount. He would top the cereal with slices of banana for extra go-get'em potassium, adding a touch of cinnamon and artificial sweetener for taste. He would have his customary 8 oz. glass of milk to the side, of course. He never counted the milk in the cereal bowl in his calcium calculations. When he felt like hot cereal, it had to be rolled oats, never processed, topped with yogurt and fresh berries.

One concession to the dark side of nutrition was his obsession with coffee. It had to be exact, which obviously meant *perfect*. While Josh prided himself in his ability to live cheaply, with no thought to fashion or comfort, he couldn't bring himself to simply scrape by on food or coffee. As you already learned, Josh was very particular about his breakfast. He was equally committed to all food. It had to be organic, locally grown, and properly prepared. His friends had long grown tired of listening to his rants about the plague of obesity inflicted on the country.

That said, he was even *most* particular about his coffee. He went deep in debt one year to buy a 'Bunn-O-Matic', the kind with hot water always at the ready. "You just put the coffee in the funnel, poured in the water, and in three minutes, you have a perfectly brewed pot of coffee at the perfect temperature, with no hinky aftertaste that comes with every other coffee maker sold at the supermarkets," he would argue to the point of being breathless.

This morning he was standing at the sink, wearing only a T-shirt: hairy ass exposed, and genitalia compacted on the other, as if seeking the warmth of his insides. He drew water for the brewer and began the ritual of carefully measuring out the precise amount of coffee into the filter. Three deliberate scoops.

He usually borrowed a friend's car and drove to the next city to buy a certain, very special, brand. It wasn't available at the food markets or super stores. He would make the trip once a month and return with the packages carefully wrapped. He stored them just as carefully, safeguarding the freshness by storing it in a location that wasn't too hot or too cold. He wanted it at its peak when the perfectly hot water started seeping through the grounds.

He rinsed out his cereal bowl this morning and poured his first cup of coffee. He always permitted himself three cups—

two more than he knew was allowed in his nutrition guide. He carried his first cup over to the table and placed it next to Remy the remington. His laptop was still asleep. He tapped on the space bar and muttered, "Wake up my pet."

While he savored his first sip of coffee, he quickly read the news on the screen. He didn't check his e-mails (mostly spam anyway). Spam was always plentiful in his inbox, despite his prolific efforts to thwart that particular evil. Just as he was about to close the cover, he noticed an ad on the right side of the webpage.

What the hell is NANOWRIMO?

His curiosity often led him down some interesting high-ways, and this was no exception. Within minutes, he was registered to write a novel—in one month, no less—a month that was starting in...he glance at the calendar...just three days. He had absolutely no idea why he just did that. How could he write a novel of 50,000 words in only 30 days?

What made this all the more curious and insensible was the reality that Josh had never written *anything* other than school papers in his entire life. He had never written a poem or a short story, let alone an entire novel. He was also pretty convinced he didn't have a very good imagination. Why had he just signed up to write a novel? And, more to the point, what in the heck would it be about?

He didn't take drugs, smoke either kind of cigarette, or alter his mind in anyway other than the high of exercise when he rode his bike. Nothing could explain this very un-Josh-like maneuver. This was moving beyond curious into the world of downright bizarre.

His mind raced with the challenge—50,000 words in 30 days? *That meant at least 1,667 words a day,* he realized, approximately 300 words per page, a mere 5.56 pages per day. Josh was prone to mentally listing negatives and positives of every action and reaction in his life.

He always started with the negatives—they were easier to come up with.

He lacked imagination.

He had no idea what to write about.

He had no idea what a plot was supposed to be, let alone a sub-plot.

He realized he knew next to nothing about novels. (He made a mental note to 'Google' novels).

He also realized this project would take time, a precious commodity for us all, even at the best of times. Josh especially could ill-afford to put his studies on hold just to write some dumb novel.

Then, the final insult registered with him: Who would ever want to read it when it was done? Worse, if they did read it, would they laugh at his effort?

Next, he turned to the positives. He sat there for a moment trying to think of one. He was positive that he only had negatives.

"You can type—that should help." Kelsey quietly came into the kitchen without Josh realizing it. She was looking over his shoulder at the computer, where he had started typing out his list of pros and cons without even realizing it.

He realized she was teasing him. "You are going to write a novel? Now that is a *novel* idea."

"Okay, Ms. English major, how hard is it?"

"You're kidding, right?"

"Dead serious," he said back.

"I started one," she said as if embarrassed. "It just sits there and stares at me, accusing me of abandonment. I've worked on it for years and still..." She just shrugged her shoulders, letting the thought die as had the novel.

"I'm in over my head, eh? Is that what you're saying?"

"I'm late for class," Kelsey said. She ran out the door and Josh looked with disdain at her disappearing back. "You never eat your breakfast," he called out after her.

The door closed and Josh was alone in the kitchen. Just Josh and Remy, and they were about to become best friends forever.

chapter

EIGHT

Josh sat staring through the window. The clouds were being swept away by a blustery late October wind, and the sun was beginning to take charge of the sky. He couldn't enjoy the view; the thought of the novel challenge was blanking out any enjoyable thoughts.

His first coffee gave way to the second. He was pouring the third when he was forced to admit he didn't have a clue how to go about doing this novel thing. Not knowing what to do was something he couldn't accept, it was like a red cloth waved in front of a fighting bull. The challenge drove him to action.

He later said he didn't know why, but he was drawn to the hat, lying quietly, patiently, on the radiator cover. Josh walked over and picked it up. As soon as he did, he felt that odd sensation again. It wasn't warmth exactly, although it resembled heat, you just couldn't quite describe the sensation. It was more an impression of magnetism, as if the hat *wanted* to attach itself to his hand. Ridiculous, of course, but there it was.

Josh drew his hand away, setting the hat back in its place. Then, he picked it up again, a reluctant acceptance washing over him. For some reason, he turned the inside leather band down and saw a small piece of paper folded up and hidden underneath. He carefully unfolded the scrap, the paper slightly brittle with age. It was a reporter's pass. He looked at the date on the ID: 1940. Somewhere along the passage of time, water must have seeped in; the ink bled away any hope of reading the signature scribbled there. All he knew was that he was holding a hat that used to belong to a reporter.

Once again, Josh cautiously put the hat on his head, imitating the look he saw in the movie last night. He was Joel McCrea as a reporter in...

1940? The thought dangled there in the air around him.

Nah, he thought, *I can't be.*

He walked over to the mirror. The hat looked authentic, a reporter's hat. The only image in the mirror that didn't look authentic was Josh; no writer of words was he. Suddenly, the tug of words started to swirl inside his imagination. He had no idea where these things were coming from.

He tried to sort out the words into some semblance of order: stones, a river, a woman, baby, animals of some sort, raptors soaring overhead, and other disparate images skittered through his mind.

What's going on? I'm losing it here.

He felt his head beginning to prickle. It had to be the hat. Words began to leap through the air in front of him, and he knew they were looking for a home. It was as though he could almost reach out and grab them with his hand. He pulled out a pile of blank sheets of paper, inserting one into the typewriter. As his hands poised over the keyboard, his fingers suddenly started typing of their own volition. He looked down at the page: the same words as the other night.

"Cold Stones in the Water," and he suddenly realized it was the title.

He looked at a pile of papers and found what he typed before. It was the beginning of a story. He pulled out the piece of paper trapped in place against the Remington's black cylinder and replaced it with the last page he been typing the previous night.

He gulped coffee and resumed typing the story banging around in some unconscious part his brain, the origins of which he was unaware.

His fingers were merely the tools of the process, a process that even bypassed the knowin parts of his brain. It felt like the story was coming from the hat, through the top of his head, down the sides of his scalp and skull, through his arms and fingers, and spewing out to the keyboard.

To test the theory he took the hat off and his fingers stopped working. He put the hat back on and the words started to flow again, like water in a stream, unstoppable.

He was typing a story about cold stones in the water, and had absolutely no idea what that meant...yet. Josh watched the words, amazed at their strength and clarity. They transported him back in time, to a place before cities, machines—almost prehistoric. It was unlike anything he had any personal awareness of. The words described a time and place he never heard of or read about.

He had the good sense to get out of the way of the words, letting them tell the story on their own. At least they seemed to know what the story was about. His brain hadn't the foggiest clue.

The story began with a young woman, lying in a shallow river, the water rushing over her. She was trembling with cold and fear. The rushing water wasn't cleansing, and it did nothing to hide the fear trembling through her body.

chapter

NINE

He's coming, she knew. That was the thought from which her fear blossomed. *They are all looking for me. They think I belong to him. They will take me back. I will never let that happen.*

She rubbed her stomach, feeling the life growing there. She leaned back again, starting to give in to the embrace of the water, letting it draw her to the white light of death. It would be so easy to give in. She almost succumbed to the siren call of that brightest light when the baby prompted her with a sudden, violent kick. That kick saved both of their lives. With a dazed grunt, she pushed herself up, lifting her body out of the cold water. The pebbled floor of the river was uncomfortable on her feet, but she carefully stepped over, using the larger ones until she reached the bank.

As she stumbled her way to dry land, she remembered falling, trying to ford the river. The knot on the back of her head must have come from a fall, she thought.

It wasn't a cold day exactly, but the temperature was dropping and she knew it would be dark soon. Cold would be an even worse enemy to her now than the man—those men, to be precise—were chasing her, following her tracks through the landscape.

That's why she crossed this river, to hide her tracks, at least for a while. They would spend a significant amount of time searching both sides of the river, looking for her tracks to appear again. It was inevitable that they would pick them up; she didn't have the skill necessary to hide all the footprints and broken leaves and branches her passing would leave behind.

She wrapped the cloth around her and walked into the brush until she was out of sight in a small copse. She ignored the deep scratches on her left arm, the blood seeped, a scarlet-ribboned gift of a thorny branch she encountered.

She walked up a small hill and looked in all directions; no sight of anyone in pursuit. Just ahead, in the growing darkness, she spotted a rabbit. With a deft and practiced hand, she pulled a smooth stone out of the bag at her side and threw it at the dumb animal. Soon, she had skinned the rabbit and left it hanging on a limb, until the bloodletting was complete.

She twirled a hardwood twig, sparking and igniting a pile of wood shavings she set in a shallow bowl hollowed out in the earth. She was her clan's fire-maker and would be sorely missed.

But this night, she used her skill to good advantage. She knew how to make a fire with minimal smoke, although it was getting dark and would be difficult to see, with only a quarter-moon riding in the sky. She reached up and took the rabbit from the branch and speared it with another piece of wood, using it as a skewer. Once it was roasted and the meat cooked inside the crispy skin, she closed her teeth onto the hindquarter and wiped the drippings from her chin as she ate. The food reawakened and strengthened her determination. She had to survive, for herself as well as for the sake of the new life growing in her.

She wrapped the uneaten rabbit in a pouch, saving it for the next morning, or perhaps a mid-day meal, depending on how her luck ran, as she made her way away from her pursuers.

She ignored the rocks and twigs on the ground as she curled her body into a protective coil, legs drawn up as close as her belly would allow. She paid no attention to animal or crawling sounds around her. As fire-starter of her clan, she was at one with the natural world and knew the creatures around her, both big and small, would leave her alone, unharmed. They would all share the night in harmony.

The woman with no name actually had a name. It was customary to assign names by function. In her language, she was called Blaze. Hers was one of the most important jobs in any clan; she was the keeper of the flame. As the clan travelled, she would protect the fire, making sure it was ever available when needed. Fire was necessary for food and warmth, especially as they moved north, where cold and snow were common in winter. Fire was warmth; fire was life.

She knew how to carry the flame as they travelled, but she also knew how to start a new fire if anything were to happen—a sudden wind or rain storm to snuff the life out of the flame.

Her mother passed along the skill to Blaze before her death five winters ago, recounting how she learned it from her own mother, who died before Blaze was born.

With a mental start, Blaze suddenly realized she could no longer remember what her mother looked like. She could see the brown hair and hazel eyes, but her mother's face was blurred with time and the hardships that passed since her death.

With a new life growing in her, Blaze realized it would soon be her turn to pass the skill along, as she was determined the child in her would be a daughter.

How did it all go wrong?

She thought back, wondering how many sunrises and sunsets passed since that fateful day.

⌒⌒

She shuddered at the memory of the man leading them suddenly turning and looking back at her. "You're holding us up woman," he grunted.

She tried to walk faster without dropping the flame bowl. Yet, she slipped on the sloping grass as she made her way down the dew-slicked hill. Attempting to protect the precious gift hidden away within her belly, she dropped the bowl and the flame sputtered away. At first, she wasn't overly concerned about the matter, until she realized there was nothing lying about suitable for fire making. The recent rains dampened the ground, leaving no dry twigs, brush or grasses. She reached into the sack she always carried and realized with a panic that she neglected to refill her supply of starter wood. She hung her head in shame for the rest of the day's journey. Since she was with child, her thoughts were on the coming birth and wandered away from her clan duties, feeling her usefulness slipping away.

They all grumbled that night, no fire for food or warmth. The animal hunter's woman was especially unpleasant in her complaining. "We need a new fire maker."

Blaze heard some grunts of agreement from other members of the clan.

She slept fitfully that night. If she were replaced as the fire maker, she would have no other skills to offer. The consequences were chilling. Outcasts were driven away, and life expectancy without a clan for protection was very short. Other clans shied away from outcasts, even those with fire-starting abilities.

⁓

The memory of that humiliation faded into the night. Alone, with the cold, lumpy ground for a mattress, Blaze made a vow to her unborn child. They would survive. It would be a promise, however, that would prove hard for her to keep.

She roused from sleep at first light and used her skills to light a "smokeless" fire. It wasn't completely smokeless, however. No fire could ever be. A sharp-eyed young man in the scouting party was pissing against the side of a tree when he spotted the faintest wisp of smoke off to the west.

"EEEYAA," he yelled.

The other five men jumped up from various degrees of sleep and quickly rolled up their belongings and headed west at a quick trot. There was no need to break into a sprinting run, yet. After all, they were confident they could easily outrun a pregnant woman.

chapter

TEN

Josh felt perspiration forming on his head; a drop started its journey from his brow, sliding lower on his cheek. He took off the fedora to wipe the sweat away and the words stopped churning in his brain. He sat motionless and pondered. He put the hat back on; the words started coming. He took the hat off; they stopped.

He put the hat on and off several times. The same result each time: hat on—words, hat off—no words. Josh was starting to feel very nervous. His anxiety fought with his breakfast for control of his stomach. It felt like his anxiety was winning the battle and was, in fact, turning quickly into a barely disguised form of fear.

Why isn't Kelsey here now? He reached for his cell phone and realized she was in class, her phone would be on 'do not disturb'. Instead of dialing, he thumbed a text, *"Help...911."* He placed the phone on the table and leaned back in the chair to wait.

He placed the hat on the typewriter. It looked jaunty, as if it belonged there. It was so cool looking, but he was starting to feel afraid of that fedora. Josh picked it up and quickly carried it by the brim with his thumb and forefinger and set it on the kitchen counter, sunlight shining through the window, and shadows from the hat splayed over the wall next to the hat. In the play of shadow and light, the hat took on a malevolent look in Josh's mind; yet at the same time, it had a mysterious look that wasn't completely unfriendly. *Curious,* he thought, *malevolent and friendly, two words that are diametrically opposed.*

Josh was a genius, of course, but his big brain simply was not equipped to explain the unexplainable. He was facing a mystery here. Puzzles of logic and cause and effect were all well and good, but an honest-to-God mystery was well beyond his logical grasp. Something inexplicable was happening to him, something he just could not wrap his brilliant mind around.

His scientific thought processes drew him to study the hat. He didn't believe in science fiction, ghosts, otherworldly events, goblins, or whatever word you gave them. He knew, deep down, there was always a logical explanation for every single event that had ever faced mankind. Yet, an explanation was proving to be elusive now. He continued to stare at the hat on the counter, willing the powers-that-be to show some sign, some indication of what was happening to him.

His phone started to vibrate, almost skating across the table in its excitement. He grabbed it, checked the caller ID, hit the green button and yelled, "It's the hat, Kelsey"

He listened a moment and said, "I *am* calm." But, he wasn't and knew it was a lie.

"I put the hat on and there are words. Then, there are no words when I take it off." He clenched the phone as he listened to Kelsey's smooth, logical calm.

"No, I haven't been drinking. I'm making perfect sense. You're not listening-"

He realized she had flipped her phone closed and stared at his own phone in disbelief. Not given to expressing fits of rage, he suddenly threw it against the kitchen wall as hard as he could. Shattered plastic exploded in all directions, and electronic parts dangled like guts from the main body lying on the floor by his foot. Staring at the disemboweled phone gave him that Peaceful Easy Feeling only *The Eagles* could ever put into words, the way they did in a song.

He knew he would not be going to his class today. He already knew as much as the professor anyway. They both agreed on that fact. It was a history class, which was a subject that actually intrigued Josh. His spongy brain could instantly absorb and memorize all the important dates, categorizing them and assigning the details to a particular order. All you needed to do was say something like August 12th, 1938 and Josh could tell you that nothing of real importance happened on that date, but he happened to know that August 12 was the birthday of Adolf Hitler's mother and that on that day in 1938, Hitler had instituted the "Mother's Cross" campaign to encourage German women to have more children. Useless piece of knowledge, but one never knew when useless information might come in handy.

His flaw was in not knowing *how* to use all the information accumulated by his brain. Raw data was important in history, but historians processed far more, wrapping that raw data into an understandable and meaningful context. Professors had the advantage in their ability to take facts and figures and numbers and weave them into a meaningful story, making dates and context come alive.

With a start, Josh realized the story he was writing was a part of history. It was a story so old it preceded history. He realized he might be channeling a story that happened long before records were ever kept, either verbally or in words or paintings.

Josh made a tentative move to the counter and picked up the fedora, determined to see the thing through. He had to know. He had to find out what was happening. He put the hat on, embracing the warm, tingling glow that came over him and shuffled back to the typewriter with a new sense of purpose.

His hands shook slightly as he inserted the next blank sheet of paper. He closed his eyes for a moment, took a deep breath, opened his eyes, and let his fingers do the walking. A story from beyond memory needed telling, and Josh realized he somehow, for some reason, was chosen to tell it. He decided not to question the how or why any more. Though he was a man reluctant to give up control of any situation, he now yielded to the idea of being an instrument, a connection to some long-forgotten woman and her child-to-be. It was a story passed to him under the broad brim of the fedora, channeled through him to his fingers, and from there, to the keys of a Remington-Rand typewriter a quarter of a century old.

chapter

ELEVEN

Blaze was tired. It had been more than three nights since she slipped around the bramble that fenced the campsite and begun her trek away from the clan. Despite her resolve, the journey was harder than she imagined.

Stargazer was a man who remained apart from the rest of the clan. He would sit for hours wrapped in a warm skin-coat. He would sit, eyes open, always watching something in the far distance, something that eluded his companions. Nobody bothered him or asked him to do chores. He was not asked to hunt or to cure hides. He accepted the small presentations of food that the members of the clan left for him, and when he did speak, he would tell whoever was listening that he didn't need much to eat.

His eyes would come alive, however, whenever the small children would come to him. They were drawn to this hermit-like man, knowing he would whisper the most wondrous stories into their willing ears whenever the whim would take hold of him. He would describe curious creatures in the star patterns of the night sky, pointing his finger into the night to trace their designs.

"See," he would say, pointing, "if you look closely at that group of stars you can see the form of a bear. My grandfather told me about it before Mother Earth took him back to the mud." Then he would sit back and enjoy the squeal of delight as the boys and girls saw the image he drew in their minds.

Blaze walked by Stargazer one day, not long before she began her lonely journey. He was sitting; legs crossed, and seemed to be absorbed in some form of meditation. It startled her when he whispered her name, "Fire Starter." She barely heard the words, they were so faint. "Sit awhile. I need to talk to you."

Intrigued, Blaze threw her bundle aside and knelt down, sitting on the ground facing him. As he talked, she had to lean in to hear his hushed words.

"That time is at hand for me."

Blaze knew what he meant. It was the way they described death.

"But, surely you can't know this. Only the wise ones can hear the calling of the mud in the earth." Though she said it, she also knew in her heart that there were some people who knew their time was at hand, if they listened to the sounds of the earth and paid attention to the signs. She leaned in, waiting for his response.

"There is no one else now but me. Who will be able to interpret the stars, to help guide the people? I tried to tell the elders and the Wise One. I tried to warn them that another must be sought. But, they turn their faces away, thinking I will be here forever." Blaze did not comment; she could see he would continue his speech.

"My father learned about the stars from his father, who learned about the stars from his father. Who knows how far that goes back?" His eyes closed and Blaze wondered if he was slipping away, to sleep or...something else.

"I am not supposed to share my knowledge with any-one not of my blood. Our laws say so. If I do, I must be put to death—to be stoned and left to die, food for the wild things. But if I am no longer here, there will be nobody to lead the way to food or shelter. We must always keep moving, constantly feeding on plants and animals as we go."

Blaze realized she wasn't expected to say anything. She looked up at him and realized just how old he was. In a world where the life cycle was very short, Stargazer was an obvious exception to that rule.

"Listen closely, child." His words were faint and even be-came fainter. "Someone has to know the secrets of the stars. Just like you needed to know the secret of fire. Everyone thinks you have some kind of magic when it comes to fire. They think the same of me, and how I can look at the stars and say turn this way or that. They expect me to point the way and tell them how long it will take us to get where we must go."

Blaze knew what he meant but remained silent.

"I have decided, Fire Starter. I have decided to pass along the secrets to you. But, you have to promise me something in return."

She nodded and whispered a quiet, "Yes, I promise. I know what you are asking, without the telling. I know how dangerous it is for both of us, sharing this knowledge."

He smiled, the first time she had ever known him to do so. "We can't be plain about it. When we talk, it must appear as nothing more than a talk about the weather. But I know you are a quick student. I have been watching you grow and learn and I see your eyes watching."

That discussion began the strange relationship between the man who could steer by the stars and the woman who could make fire for food and warmth.

Days passed into weeks, until one day Stargazer announced, "You have been the perfect student. You are ready now. I have passed along my knowledge of the stars and my job is done." It was dark as he looked up, a crooked finger poking at the heavens. "Everyone else looks up and only sees a canvas of lights. To you, they are now beacons that call you to faraway places, places of refuge." He began to cough. "The stars will guide you if follow their lead. Let them take you to the heavens of our world."

She started to thank him, to say something to show how grateful she was to be honored with his knowledge.

"You are going to have a child." He paused. "It will be dangerous for you. There are people who want you to pass your fire skills to a different family. They want to control your knowledge, to have it interpreted in their own way. I have heard them talk."

She looked at him in alarm. She was feeling the warmth of the child growing inside her more every day now, allowing her to ignore the cold roughness of the coupling she endured with the clan leader. She wondered why he had taken her into the darkness and forced himself on her that night, never to claim her in the daylight hours as he did his other women.

"There is a plan to wait until the child is born. You will be killed and the child will be taken by others."

She sat before him, slack-jawed. Could she believe what she just heard? But, it was something she suspected. Not the details she was hearing now, but the quiet whispers and pointed looks by the elders told her that her future with the clan was tentative at best.

"My time is soon," he said. "While they pretend to mourn my passing, you must make your move. You must steal your chance for life and run. We are all afraid of being alone, but you have fire, and now you have the stars to guide you. They will have neither. Our leader thinks he knows the ways of fire, but he is only fooling himself. Hunter thinks he can read the stars, but he never listened to me when he was a child, and he doesn't hear me now. He thinks he knows, and that ignorance will kill him in the end, and the rest of the clan who will follow without thinking."

"I will miss you Stargazer," she said hoarsely, her eyes filling with tears. She could hardly see him through the filmy teardrops, but she felt the warmth of his chest as he wrapped an arm around her and drew her close.

"It will happen soon, daughter. It will be over as it should be. Remember me when you look up at the heavens." He pointed out a grouping of stars, a grouping he never mentioned before.

She saw it then. It was the outline of the face of an old man, beard clearly visible.

"I will always be looking up at you Stargazer." Kissing him lightly on the cheek, she rolled her blanket and returned to her fire ring.

The next day, people erupted in a loud keening. Stargazer was dead. "I am ready to take over," Hunter said. The looks of the clan showed few believed he could. Yet, they knew there was no choice. There was no one else.

There was a three day ritual of the dying. On the first day, the women cleaned the corpse and prepared it with balms and herbs. Stargazer looked peaceful in repose.

The second day, everyone sat around a large fire and shared stories of him. Old men remembered listening to his stories when they were children. The small children wept openly, their kindly story teller gone forever. They knew death; death surrounded them and they knew it wasn't a journey from which there was no way back.

On the third day, the men lit a large fire. It was a funeral pyre meant to consume Stargazer with the warmth of Mother Earth, burning like the sun, leaving nothing for the wild things to desecrate. The elders claimed the smoke rising from the pyre carried the soul of Stargazer to join his ancestors amongst the stars, but only a handful of that group actually believed.

Blaze listened to the men making plans to scavenge for wood, knowing she would create the needed fire. It had to be the right kind—wood that burned long and very hot. They knew from experience just how hard it was to burn a body completely; reducing it to ashes with only the smallest clumps of bone.

Blaze heard the men walking into the darkness to gather wood and quietly packed up her blanket, preparing to sneak away, looking around to see if anyone noticed. No one else stirred. It was the time of year when darkness came early and left late. It was the season they called "snows leaving."

She walked west and then north, glancing up to let the stars guide her. She walked farther and farther through the night. When she checked the stars, she always made sure to smile at the image of Stargazer watching over her. She was thankful for his wisdom and his eternally vigilant gaze. She knew she would never be completely alone as long as his star-face burned in the sky.

As the sun in the east gradually turned the inky darkness to a slate grey, people back in the camp slowly came awake.

"What happened to the fire?" someone asked.

"Get Blaze," another said.

"Where is she?"

"We don't have any fire."

"What are we going to do?"

"Where is Blaze?"

The huge man they called their leader heard the wails and realized that the suspicion he harbored over the last few weeks was confirmed. He watched Blaze and the Stargazer together. Now he was sure the old man taught her the secret star map. The plan he had for the baby she was carrying, his child, was to replace her as the fire starter. Now the plan was going suddenly gone awry.

"We don't have time to whine and moan," he yelled. "Quickly, I want the five best hunters. Now! We are going after our fire starter. She must be found and returned. She has to give us the child and the secrets she holds."

Wide eyes stared frightened at the huge man in bear skin. No one argued with the leader.

They wanted their fire back.

chapter

TWELVE

Josh took off the hat and looked at his watch. *Has that much time passed? I have to know where and when this story is coming from. I can't seem to pinpoint the time or place. Who can I find that would know?*

He decided that a break was in order. He needed to clear his head. He also needed a new cell phone before Kelsey got wind of his earlier temper tantrum. He looked at his bicycle leaning against the closet door. He checked the temperature on the thermometer hanging outside the kitchen window and pulled on a sweatshirt, the one with a hood. He rolled the bike to the elevator and reached under the handlebar to lift it upright, balancing it on the rear wheel. He was able to guide it into the elevator and still leave room for others.

He pushed the bike out through the lobby and began to ride down the street. He felt a calm returning to his body as his muscles took up the challenge. He felt the wind in his face, refreshing, cooling. He tried to forget the fedora lying next to Remington on the kitchen table.

He enjoyed the release he got from the story flowing through him. The farther he rode, the more relaxed he became. Released from the grip of the story, he a thought of his own. One of the professors at school, whom he didn't know personally, was reportedly an expert in prehistory. He had written papers on peoples that long ago disappeared from memory: peoples in the great deserts of the American Southwest, nomadic peoples who travelled from the cold of northern Europe to the warmth of the Mediterranean Sea, people in search of climate that would provide food, plant and animal.

That was it! He would arrange an introduction and share his strange story, part of it, anyway. He would ask if it made any sense, from a historic point of view, of course.

The decision made, Josh realized he was on the same street where he found that odd store advertising cheap stuff. He remembered some of the details. He recalled the cheap stuff store was sandwiched between the dry cleaning store and the meat market, somewhere close to the hardware store. *Right there!*

But, there wasn't a store, only a laneway that went back to an alley in the rear.

I am absolutely sure, he thought.

There was the fence railing where he clearly remembered chaining his bike. *There,* he remembered. Over there was the place he had tried to balance the heavy typewriter, dropping the bike against the retaining wall as he ran back to the store to buy the almost-forgotten fedora. That damned fedora.

He got off the bike, leaning it against the same retaining wall. He walked slowly up and down the street, no "cheap stuff" store to be seen. He turned into the laneway and walked back to the alley. He peered right and left. There was no sight of a store of any kind, let alone a cheap stuff store.

He was walking back to the street and his bicycle when he thought he heard it—a phlegmy cough. He could have sworn it was the same cough he had once heard coming out of the old man in the cardigan, the man who sold him the hat and the typewriter. But when Josh looked around, there was no one to be found.

He asked people in the meat market and dry cleaning store about the cheap stuff store and was met with blank stares. They all politely told him he was mistaken and to try the Goodwill store five blocks down and two over. He picked up the bike leaning against that same retaining wall—he was sure of it—and with one last look behind him, he rode slowly back to the apartment.

On his way home, he remembered to pick up another phone. *So much for being thrifty,* he thought. Though, he couldn't honestly say he regretted his earlier fit of temper. For a split second in his life, it felt good to lose control. Pocketing the new phone, he slipped the bicycle into the elevator and finally pushed it through the door of the apartment.

He leaned the bike against the closet door and lifted the sweatshirt over his head, tossing it over the back of the sofa. He turned to the kitchen. Remington and that damned hat were still there, waiting. Josh felt the beginning of a headache, one he knew was not going away any time soon. He carefully put his new phone on the table and swept up the pieces of the old one, burying them deep in the trash can.

Making sure he had the same number, his phone now lit up with a text message: "B home @ 7:00—2 veggie subs and coke. luv, K."

He picked up the fedora, placed it on his head and stared at it in the mirror. He put the reporter's ID card in the band, giving the hat a rakish look. It was the pose he imagined a reporter would have struck back in the day. He tugged the brim down to shield his eyes from the bare overhead light bulb. It was a gesture he saw Bogart use in *Casablanca*.

For some reason, he no longer felt anxiety or fear when he put on the hat. His curiosity was taking over. He wanted to know; he *had* to know. His fingers were poised over the keys; a fresh sheet of paper was wrapped around the platen. He was ready.

chapter

THIRTEEN

Blaze, the fire starter, never felt so alone. She was used to living in a clan. They worked collectively, each person with a specialized task to perform and everyone with a place. No individual stood alone, apart from the group. Even the clan leader relied on others in the clan, like the fire starter and the stargazer. The leader was only the first among equals; he was afforded no special powers by the gods.

Yet, even in such an idealistic-sounding society, internecine squabbling always developed. The collective was comprised of several family groups, their DNA threading common characteristics, some better than others.

She was not been prepared to be on her own, to be responsible for more than starting and maintaining a fire. Her fear was palpable in the morning light. At the same time, a flush of exhilaration washed over her. She felt suddenly unleashed from the collective spirit. She looked up at the rising sun and started to laugh. It was the first time she ever heard the sound of her own laughter fill the air.

She never knew what made her turn around, but she saw the merest speck of dust on a hill in the distance behind her. It was too far away to have any definition, but her instincts told her it was a man's mark, not an animal. They were coming, she knew.

She pushed down the feeling of panic and imposed calmness over her mind and body. She recalled the position of the stars just before the night sky gave way to the day. She was headed northward, just to the west of north. She looked in that direction now, imposing mountain tops rising in the morning heat. They had a rippling appearance, a result of the sun's warming rays meeting the coolness of the earth.

She made a quick calculation and decided to turn more to the north, slightly away from the direction the dust devils seemed to be heading. *That will give them something to think about,* she thought as she stepped into another stream and waded through the ankle-deep water. *They won't be able to follow these footsteps.* She smiled.

She followed the stream for some distance, clearly tracking out of the water and up the bank for a ways, through some dry brush. She backtracked in her own prints, back to the water, crossed back over the stream and then stepped up on the dry bank, carefully planting her feet on rocks or where the earth was hard-packed and resisted the imprint of her feet. She found a clump of bushes several yards away from the stream and squatted, fading back until she was invisible to anyone passing by.

She waited.

She waited.

She waited.

She heard them before she saw them.

Some hunters, she thought. *The animals can hear them from a mile away with the noise they make.*

"I see the track," hunter shouted. They definitely were giving no thought to stealth. "There," said one, and she imagined him pointing right at her.

She heard them laughing. "How did she expect to get away with this? Imagine, Blaze, the fire-starter trying to outwit hunters." She heard them thrashing through the underbrush. She closed her eyes tight, waiting, and not daring to breathe. She heard the voices fade as they followed the tracks she made away from her hiding spot until they came to the stream.

"Spread out. She must have crossed here. Look for her tracks on the other side."

She felt her leg cramping but willed the pain away, keeping silent in her hiding place. She felt a gentle kicking in her stomach and rubbed the spot, praying for the new one to be quiet.

"Where?"

"I don't know."

"I think I see something."

"She is heading that way. She won't get far, now."

It was their arrogance leading them away from her hiding spot. They couldn't believe a woman possessed the skill to outwit them in the hunting game. She was no panicked grouse or rabbit. She was the Blaze, the fire starter and Stargazer had given her the map, a map leading her away from those who would take her life and steal her child. All she had to do was remain calm and wait, and she was good at waiting. Fire always required patience.

The sun passed over the high point and was dropping toward the western horizon when Blaze felt safe enough to move from her hiding place. It was a long time since she heard the men, so sure of themselves, so sure they would catch her. She stood, stretched, and scanned in all four directions. There was no sign of the men.

She was glad she still had some rabbit meat left in her pouch. It would mean another meal, energy and inner fire for another night alone. Breakfast would be another story. There would be no fire this time. She turned and once again headed to the northwest; a special mountain top in the distance drew her like a magnet.

Just as she turned, she heard a terrible sound. It was the burring of a snake, the one with a rattle. It was nearby and she immediately recognized the danger. She had forgotten there was more to fear out here in the wild than the hunters.

Freezing, she stopped in mid-stride, her right leg ready to step ahead, now poised in mid-air. She saw it then, the snake. It was coiled and hissing its warning at her. When she didn't move, the snake seemingly decided she was no threat. She later would swear the snake winked at her as it uncoiled and lazily slithered its way in search of more appropriate food. Blaze was too big to be a comfortable meal for the rattler.

It was a close encounter, for certain, but Stargazer had told her something important: You have only to fear the animals on two legs. You don't need to be as afraid of those creatures that walked on four legs. He told her to listen to what they told her, that they could help her on her journey.

"Take what you need for food and sustenance," he told her. "Live in harmony with the rest." It was a lesson that would serve her well in the time ahead. Even the snake, venom ready, meant her no harm; it meant only to protect itself, to live to see another warm meal. And so she walked on, a little less afraid than before.

Farther away, the leader finally turned to hunter. "Where is the Fire Starter? Where did she go? You are supposed to be the best hunter and you can't even find her trail," he growled, cuffing the man with the back of his hand. It wasn't a friendly tap, and Hunter knew he disappointed the leader. He had earned his shame.

There was no choice but to return to the river and retrace their steps. Much daylight had been lost and Hunter would now carry this shame until the fire starter was found and returned to the clan. He had been the one who made the decision to look downriver. It was a mistake that cost them valuable time. Had they turned upriver instead, they might have picked up her trail sooner. It was three days before they all agreed that she outwitted them.

Almost ten sunrises more took place when they found the first faint trace of her trail. The youngest tracker spotted something in the brush where she hid that day, on the side of the river opposite of where they expected. It was the merest trace of an indentation, where her knee touched the ground as she waited. It was enough to give them pause. She had been clever, more than any of them expected. Hunter acknowledged the find, praising the young tracker for his keen sense. He looked toward the path where Blaze made her way through the brush, seeing the mountains in the distance. "We need Stargazer now."

The leader looked at him with rage. "We will find her, Stargazer or not."

chapter

FOURTEEN

The apartment was far from soundproof and Josh often listened to the neighbors having one of their infamous fights. It was a reminder that the yelling between him and Kelsey didn't go unnoticed. When he heard the soft "bing" of the elevator, he looked at his watch and knew Kelsey was home. He couldn't wait to tell her about his discovery regarding Remington and the hat.

He should have known after all this time that Kelsey would also have a few things to talk about. Her day was important, too. Unfortunately, 'Kelsey's day' was a concept that often escaped Josh, much to his own peril.

The door was still closing when he pounced. "Kelsey, you wouldn't believe-"

"I can't believe that my advisor is such a total ass." He should have known by her glare that now was the time to shut up. But sometimes when you have a brain as big as Josh, important things get lost in all that space.

"Wait, it isn't as important as what happened to me today!" Those were words Josh would later regret. This wasn't an IKEA commercial he could talk over. Kelsey's glare turned to white-hot rage, and she began yelling at Josh at a decibel level that rivaled an aircraft carrier, jet engines fully engaged. He backed away from her fury into the apartment, eyes and mouth wide in utter shock.

"You inconsiderate selfish ass!" she shouted. "You are the most self-centered bastard I've ever known! How *dare* you have the *balls* to tell me your day was more important than mine when I can tell all you've done today was lay around and do absolutely NOTHING!"

She threw the bag at him. He didn't duck in time, and the content of the veggie subs painted the walls with tomatoes, lettuce and a vinegar/oil combination that was a putrid grey color. Josh stood in the middle of the kitchen with an array of lettuce clumped on his shoulder.

"You didn't have to do that." It was a useless statement. In fact, it only served to make her more irate. Kelsey turned and stormed into the bedroom. The door slammed shut with a decisiveness that was a record, even for her. Nine-point-O on the Richter scale, he was sure.

"I didn't get to tell you about-" he stopped as his own words echoed back from the closed door. This wasn't the first time this fight had taken place. Probably wouldn't be the last, either, knowing Josh's tendency to stick his foot in his mouth.

Josh turned and started picking up the assorted parts of the subs that had been so unceremoniously been flung about. He picked up the larger pieces and dropped them in the trash. Then, he got the broom and swept the smaller pieces into the dust pan and dumped them into the trash as well. Finally, he wiped down the wall, the counter, and the table until the evidence of Kelsey's anger was erased—much as he did with the mutilated cell phone earlier in the day. He returned the broom, and taking the mop and bucket, sponged the floor until it was shiny and clean.

He viewed his efforts as a peace offering, hoping Kelsey would appreciate the effort when she returned to her senses. But, it was just such thinking that kept rubbing her the wrong way. He was oblivious to his part in launching her tirades, which always seemed so illogical to him.

He looked over at where he left the fedora, but he didn't pick it up. Instead, he reached for his cell and called his history professor.

"I need the name of that professor who writes about prehistoric people," he said without introduction or small talk. He never did quite get it: connecting with someone before demanding something. In a way, Kelsey was right when she said he was a self-centered bastard. So many things simply did not occur to Josh, like inane pleasantries and niceties that people engaged in before getting to the point. Josh just did not think those things were necessary, and that way of thinking clearly showed through in his social skills.

He nodded while he listened, writing a name and phone number on a piece of paper. Without as much as a good-bye, he hung up, dialed the number, and waiting for an answer.

"Hello?"

"Dr. Livingston?" He bit his cheek and refrained from adding, "I presume."

It wasn't long before he was deep in conversation with the man. He told the professor the outline of the story his hat begun to lead him through.

"No," Josh said, "I don't know what will happen, yet. It sounds crazy, I know, but the story is just sort of coming to me as I go along. I'm not sure where this story is taking place and I have absolutely no idea where names like Blaze, Fire Starter and Stargazer come from."

"Such names were not unusual for the nomadic tribes of the Neolithic or pre-Proto-Indo-European periods, or even the Archaic Woodland Indians of North America. The peoples we know about, at least," Livingston said. "Names were assigned to each person, determined by the role they played in the tribe or clan."

"She talks about the leader, a man who apparently impregnated her and had many wives," Josh said.

"That was a common practice—a common breeding practice that ensured strong offspring; Darwinism at its finest." He chuckled a bit at his last comment.

Josh didn't quite think it was funny. "Well, he doesn't sound like a pleasant man."

"Tell me again," Livingston said, a hint of suspicion creeping into his voice, "how did you happen upon this story?"

Josh really didn't have an answer to that question that didn't make him sound like a total nut case. *Well, you see, I have this magic hat I bought from a store that doesn't exist...*

Unfortunately, Josh realized too late that the words he thought were only in his head actually made their way out of his mouth. There was a stunned, buzzing silence on the other end of the line.

"Who is putting you up to this?" The man on the phone demanded, obviously incapable of believing a story like this. Josh couldn't really blame him: a story being channeled from the prehistoric past through a 1940's reporter's hat. It sounded crazy to him and he was in the middle of it all, seeing it happening first-hand.

Josh listened to the click of disconnect on the other end.

"Prick," he grumbled. "He'll be the last person to hear the outcome of this story."

It was dark now, and the only light glared out from a bare bulb shining down from the ceiling fixture. He looked at the closed bedroom door. She would come out when she was good and ready, he knew. Not a minute before.

He picked through the bits and pieces of the sub, the parts salvaged from the tantrum. As he munched, his mind kept returning to the story. He wanted to know what happened next. He didn't usually drink, but this time he reached in the cupboard and pulled out a bottle of single-malt scotch, a bottle he kept for special occasions. He poured a glass, neat. It was his favorite, Glen Garioch. It was an incredibly expensive new release: distilled in 1978 and bottled just this year. He savored the peat flavor to the malt that had been missing for many years after the Japanese bought out the distillery and changed the blend.

He sipped again and savored the burning sensation as the liquid lined his throat. The drink gave off an almost bitter taste, turning to a hint of oak, and then blossomed into a delicious, smoky flavor, a process he thoroughly enjoyed.

He plugged his MP3 player in and dialed his favorite playlist: The trumpet sounds of Miles Davis. It was "Sketches of Spain," *the best song of all*, Josh thought.

He circled the table, wanting to put the hat on and get going with the story. For some reason, he was reluctant this evening; not afraid exactly, he just wanted to stretch his legs by walking about the room, taking delicate sips of his scotch.

He tilted his head back and drained the last drop of amber from the glass, rinsed it, and put it on the sink towel to dry. That done, he walked with purpose back to the table. He sat down and reached for the hat. The paper was nested between the rollers and he was ready to begin.

chapter

FIFTEEN

Blaze looked at the mountain ahead, the one with the unusual shape, the shape of a bony finger pointing up to the heavens. She suddenly remembered the finger Stargazer used to point out the stars. Thinking of him, she started to weep, soft tears washing her cheeks as she walked.

"Child, it takes more than the stars. I have a memory of shapes. A mountain shape, the shape of a particular tree, the place of the sun in the sky, the moon at night." He patiently passed all of his knowledge over to her as they talked.

I love you Stargazer. I will always treasure your gift. I will always honor the wisdom you have given me, she thought.

Love was an emotion uncommon for the people of the time. They were drawn to some members and repelled by others, but the concept of love and hate had not yet fully evolved. They needed only basic urges to survive. They needed food and sustenance. They needed to clothe themselves, and they needed shelter from the elements. Emotional attachments were a range of dynamics later humankind would experience.

Blaze wondered at the feeling, but finally set it aside and concentrated on her path toward the mountain. She walked until the sun was well past its midday point. All this way, and the mountain still seemed no closer. The only change she could even note was a slight upward slope to the ground beneath her feet.

Small trees now grew around her instead of the scraggly shrubs and bushes she struggled through before. She came to a stream of water. Instead of finding a trickle of water flowing over small stones and pebbles, this stream had steep banks and when she stepped in, her feet plunged into water that went up to her knees. Water this deep was a new experience for Blaze, and she felt a moment of panic, knowing nothing of swimming, having never needed the skill. Her life existed entirely in wandering the semi-desert and near-desert grass plains.

She had just enough meat left from a rabbit for one more small meal. She knew she would have to hunt soon. The sun plunged toward the horizon, and she stoically ignored her hunger, deciding she would wait to take her final meal of rabbit meat once she stopped for the night. In this new terrain, she wasn't sure when she would find her next meal.

Her methodical footsteps carried her higher into the low foothills. She thought the mountain now looked closer, but she wasn't sure. She felt a sudden chill, the temperature beginning to drop as she entered the hills as night approached.

Stargazer warned her about the changing climate. While there was always a wide range of temperatures on the desert floor, this was decidedly different. Untying her belongings, she draped her animal skin around her shoulders.

As she looked around, she realized there was another difference. Firewood was always scarce on the desert floor. Here, she saw more than enough for tonight's fire. She found the type of wood Stargazer described to her. It would be perfect for a fire and she could tell by its weight and texture that it would emit little smoke.

Remembering her close encounter with the hunters, she decided she would not make a fire until after dark. She could shield the flames from view and the smoke wouldn't be visible in the near-moonless night.

The sunlight faded into a moonless sky, the stars blinking a roadmap for her to follow. She finally stopped near a small stone outcropping, a nice sheltered niche on the leeward side. After digging out a shallow bowl, she built a small fire with her dried grass and kindling, feeding the larger twigs to the flames when it caught well enough. She settled herself into a comfortable position, her head resting on her belongings, the skin pulled up to give her warmth.

She pulled out the rest of the meat and savored each bite, trying not to think about the hunger that awaited her in the days ahead. She banked the fire and felt the heat from the glowing embers on her feet. She thought about Stargazer, looking at his face in the stars.

Not far away, a group of men were also taking bed for the night. The leader was in a foul mood and stayed off to the side, just on the edge of the fire's light. Hunter was talking to the two trackers. He gave them their instructions for the next day. They were to fan out in widening arcs, looking for any signs of Fire Starter. The remaining two, the beaters, knew their job without being told. They would range ahead and between the two trackers, making noise to startle their quarry into running.

This was their hunting tradition. The beaters did their job, the trackers picked up the scent, the hunter made the capture, and the leader claimed all the credit. That was the way it was supposed to be.

They were closer than they knew, but Blaze was not one to bolt from hiding. She stayed under cover when they passed her earlier in the hunt, and she knew the value of patience.

There was one flaw in their plan. They were heading in a slightly different direction, one that kept them moving nearly, but not quite, parallel to Blaze's trail, keeping Blaze out of harm's way.

That was all about to change.

chapter

SIXTEEN

Josh was curious. What was going to happen to Blaze? What was about to change? No matter how curious he was, he was just too tired to go on. His back hurt, his shoulders were aching from hunching over the table and keyboard. Typing on Remy required more strength and dexterity than he had first understood and made him ache from fingertips to the bottom of his skull.

He was developing speed on the old typewriter, however. He was growing quite fond of the Remington. There was a rhythmic sound to the typing. He found he didn't have to strike the keys as hard as at first. With use and the benefit of machinist's oil, the keys were flying under his touch, now, his fingers gaining strength. The odd thing he noticed was the letter "R". There was a slight bend in the arm extension and the letter "R" would always type a bit higher than the rest.

It wasn't quite a superscript height, but it was noticeably higher, and not quite as dark. He fiddled with the arm for a while, and finally decided it would be an idiosyncrasy that gave the manuscript character. He was amazed at the growing pages of typing, just to the left.

The rhythm of the typewriter varied with the speed Josh typed, and he was up to 50-plus words per minute and gaining speed. The keys struck the page, clackity, clackity, clackity, clackity, until the platen reached the end and the bell dinged. Josh would reach up with his left hand and drive the carriage back to the far right, advancing the page, and he would start again, clackity-clack, clackity-clack-clack-clack.

Amazing, he thought, *and this is all completely mechanical, not an electronic component anywhere. How did they ever figure it out? The inventor was quite something. I wonder how long these things have been around...*

It was time to rest for the night. His word count was growing, his fingers ached, and he needed sleep. He walked to the sink, drawing a glass of water and downing a handful of aspirin to chase away his headache.

He walked into the bathroom to piss. He remembered to put the seat down out of respect for Kelsey and her girl friends. He brushed his teeth and drew his t-shirt up over his head to throw it in the pile of dirty clothes in the corner of the bathroom. He wondered whose turn it was to make the trip to the Laundromat and vaguely thought he should probably do it regardless. Kelsey was pissed off enough as it was. It surely wouldn't hurt the situation any.

He turned out the bathroom light, and as he walked out to the kitchen, he heard the sobs coming from the bedroom. They got louder and more theatrical, and Josh recognized the ritual with a sigh and a roll of his eyes. He'd watched this scene play numerous times. She would storm into the bedroom, slam the door, and lay in bed with her hand on her forehead like the death scene in *Camille*. Not the 2007 version, but the original from 1936: star-crossed love and terminal illness and all. Then, when she was all cried out, she would start to sob—loudly. That was his cue to quietly open the door, lie down next to her and take her in his arms and apologize profusely. After stroking her arm and hair, she would finally turn, and in an instant, they would be making love—clothes and sheets and pillows kicked out of the way, strewn around the bedroom.

Tonight was no different, except the radio alarm went flying as Josh's leg sprawled out of control while they were rolling. It was probably broken beyond repair.

They both leaned back afterward, sweaty and content. Josh only wished he smoked. This was the perfect place and time for a cigarette.

Camille...

With that thought, he straightened up without warning, almost rolling Kelsey off the bed. Greta Garbo had looked stunning in that film, wearing those bold, sweeping hats tied down with a scarf. One hat was so large it looked like an alien space ship ready to pull her off into the heavens. He remembered Robert Taylor in the movie, the part where he was wearing a fedora.

Josh was wise and knew he would have to listen to Kelsey talk about the troubles in her day. He pushed Robert Taylor, Greta Garbo and the spooky tan fedora to the outskirts of his mind and tried to focus on Kelsey's problems for a change.

"Professor Spencer was just awful, Josh. He didn't like my proposal and said so in no uncertain terms. You know how I hate to start crying, especially in front of a man, but he was just..." she trailed off and took a deep, shuttering breath.

"Screw him," Josh replied.

"Then the us was late. By the time I got on, there was no place to sit. The smell was awful. Some people don't seem to know what a bath or shower is, I swear."

When she had finished venting about her day, he felt her body soften and relax, and she slowly melted into the crook of his arm. "I'm hungry. And I am sorry about the sub." When he looked down into her eyes, he knew she was sincere. He smiled at her and gently tweaked her nose.

"I saved some for you," he said, and went out to the kitchen. He came back with a plate and a bottle of beer, his peace offering over the situation.

"I want to tell you about the fedora," he finally broached the subject. He got a beer for himself and pulled up a chair next to the bed. Leaning back to balance on the back two legs; he put his feet up on the bed and started telling her all about Remington and the magical fedora.

When he finished she looked at him and idn't say a word. He waited, knowing she was often the voice of reason when chaos was reigning.

"Are you bullshitting me?"

"No," he said, offended. "Do you want to see?"

He walked out and brought back the manuscript. Handing it to her, he sat back on the chair and waited. He watched her eyes scanning the words, turning the pages and finally tossing the last page on the pile next to her.

"You really wrote this," she sounded skeptical, but it wasn't exactly a question. "I am surprised, you have quite an imagination." But she knew he was not given to imaginings. "Where did the idea come from? Wasn't there a documentary we saw that talked about something like this? That's it! It was a documentary speculating about life before known history."

But she knew from his look that he wasn't buying her theory.

"I'm telling you it's the hat, Kelsey. I put it on and I hear the story, like its being dictated to me. I take the hat off and the dictation just stops."

He got up and went into the kitchen, returning with the hat in his hand. He didn't put it on, merely carried it. The hat felt warm in his hand, but he resisted the urge put it on. Instead, he handed it to Kelsey, who scooted away in the bed, holding up her hands as though warding off some evil spirit. "I don't want to even touch that hat, let alone put it on." She later admitted to a close girl friend that she was afraid of the fedora but couldn't explain why.

Without thinking, Josh threw the hat up on the dresser and turned out the lights. He held Kelsey, sorry for the fight but happy for the make-up sex. The night felt incomplete, somehow. It was like he forgot something and it bothered him.

He sat upright and yelled, "Shit," slapping the side of his head. "I have an early class tomorrow and I almost forgot about it in all this mess."

Kelsey yawned and he watched her eyes close again, falling into a deep sleep, despite his angst. He reached for the radio alarm and realized it was shattered beyond usefulness. He picked up his cell and set the alarm. He closed his eyes and never noticed the faint glow—a greenish aura—emanating from the hat atop the dresser.

The next day, Josh hurried home from class. His photographic memory would record all the details he would need to remember about the professor's ramblings. He rushed into the apartment and yelled for Kelsey. He walked in the kitchen and saw the note on the board, the place where they usually left such notes for each other.

I think we both need a break. I haven't seen Sarah in ages, so I called her, and I'm going. I won't be gone long. I'm not pissed off or anything, honest. I just need to go shopping with a girl-

friend, eat ice cream and watch a three hankie movie. I'm turning off my cell, but I will call you to see how you and Remy are doing. Love K."

Josh read the note through again, looking for clues as to how pissed off she really was, despite her assurances otherwise. He finally decided it would have to work itself out on its own.

In the meantime, he threw his backpack on the sofa, stripped off his hoodie and looked for the fedora. Then he remembered it was in the bedroom. He felt almost like an addict looking for a fix as he put the hat on and sat down in front of Remington.

chapter

SEVENTEEN

Blaze woke up, alert to any unusual sounds. There were none. She heard animal noises, the ones you would expect to hear as night turned into day. The night creatures were busy finding a hiding place, and the day creatures were greeting the new day. It was a ritual for all of them—to find food, consume food, and then rest. It was a cycle that continued over and over again until death. Then, through birth, the cycle would start all over again.

Blaze knew that the animals and crawling things around her were also a source of nutrition for her own body. She was a part of that natural cycle of finding food, consuming it and then resting. She knew the secrets of what could and couldn't be eaten. What she hadn't known from her life with the clan was augmented by the knowledge Stargazer passed on.

With that knowledge, she looked around. There was a bush with berries. She knew it was a tart, almost bitter tasting berry, but it was edible. She picked the berries and forced herself to eat. She watched insects, an army them, trailing from a flowering plant to a dried piece of wood. She didn't have a name for them, but they were large. She started a small fire—just a few twigs. Then she used a stick to stir the piece of rotting wood, and found the insects underneath were busy converting the residue of the flower into something sweet and edible. She scooped them out by the handful, ignoring their wriggling and placing them on a bowl-shaped rock she placed amidst the coals of the fire. Once she roasted them and crunched them down, she was ready to start walking.

She carefully erased all evidence of her stay, filling in the fire bowl and brushing away her foot prints with dried brush. As she started to walk away, her foot slipped on the side of a rock and twisted. She fell to her knees with a small cry of pain. She knew at once it was a critical accident. It wasn't broken; but she knew it would turn blue and then an ugly black. Worse, she would have trouble staying ahead of the hunters.

She avoided putting weight on the ankle as best she could and looked for a nearby bush, the one with the large leaves. She soaked them in the stream and relit a small fire. After she heated the leaves, she wrapped them tightly around her ankle. She knew how dangerous this was. She didn't have any food, couldn't walk, and she was in pain.

The steamed leaves eased the pain and a curious bird landed next to her, looking up at her as if to ask what she was doing lazing around like that when the day had already begun. She reached out, survival instincts at work, and caught the bird. Wringing its neck, she placed the bird on a spit, burning away the feathers, and fell back on the ground once she consumed every piece, including the soft little bones. She put her injured ankle up on a log near the fire and it helped ease the pain even more.

The bird saved her life. She needed to conserve her energy and the bird would sustain her for a time. By the end of the next day, she could put weight on her ankle, but the pain was still almost unbearable. She fashioned a walking stick to help her bear weight. She was growing anxious; she knew she couldn't stay much here longer. The beaters and trackers would eventually come this way and she needed to be gone when they did.

She rested one more night, eased by the delight of another rabbit. Finally, she awoke on the following morning. She gathered her belongings, left-over meat from the rabbit, carefully wrapped and stored, and her direction toward the mountain was true. She started walking toward the finger rising high into the sky, its point touching the clouds today. She began to call it Stargazer Mountain in her mind.

She intended to leave no sign of her stay. She took extra care to erase all evidence of her presence. Satisfied, she broke camp and started walking to the north and west.

She was unaware that a small piece of her sandal had broken away when she fell. It was a clue that would put the hunting party back on the right path, and just as the sun went down that day, one of the beaters pointed it out to a tracker, who pointed it out to the hunter, who told the leader.

The leader looked grim and determined. "I told you she can't outwit us. We will start tomorrow at first light and this time, we will run. She's so close I can smell her."

chapter

EIGHTEEN

Josh needed a break. He was finding he could only go so long without taking the fedora off. His brain felt like it was swelling to the point it might explode, if such a thing were actually possible. It was similar to what happened when his computer sent a bunch of data to the printer. The printer would start printing, but the unprinted data remained all packed up together on the other end of the cable, cached in a file off to the side. The bits and bytes queued faster than the printer's ability to print.

The words from the fedora felt like that. They would build up while he was typing, compiling faster than he could type, pushing him, demanding he learn to type faster. He found that now when he took the hat off, the words would still flow to his fingertips, sometimes for several minutes after ripping the fedora from his head. The words would gradually peter to a trickle and then finally stop altogether. Though he resisted putting the hat back on, he really wanted to know what was going to happen to the girl.

He rubbed the top of his head and was surprised by the stubble he felt there. He remembered then, what he had done to his hair. While his idea, an impulse, might not shock and amaze anyone, young Josh displayed a full mane of hair, right down past his shoulders. Was the feeling of stubble he had on the top of his head now completely and utterly imaginary? He remembered his decidedly un-Josh-like decision earlier.

He went into the bathroom and found the clippers in a box under the sink. He set them on the countertop and went into the bedroom and found the supremely sharp little hair scissors that Kelsey always used. He returned to the bathroom and stared at the mirror for a moment or two, and then started pulling his long hair up with his left hand and cutting indiscriminately with the scissors. Clip, clip, clip. The strands of hair fell away like leaves in fall and soon littered the sink, the countertop and spread out like a fan around his feet. He kept cutting until only a modest growth was left on his head.

Then he opened the box and took out the electric hair cutter. He took off the trim guard—the number 4 clip—and started to shave down to the scalp. When he finished, he lathered his head and reached for the razor, the one Kelsey used on her legs. It wasn't the sharpest razor in the drawer, but soon his head was shaved completely to the scalp, smooth.

He showered and started to sweep up when he looked in the mirror. The image that screamed back at him reminded him of someone. Who? Then he remembered watching a rerun of an old cop show. It was Kopak, Kiljack, no...*Kojak*. That was it.

Who played Kojak? Telly Savalas. God, who could forget a name like that? Wasn't he the guy who always had a lollipop in his mouth? Wasn't he the one who always said, "Who loves ya, baby?" That's *who I freaking look like.*

And an eerie thought washed through him: the Kojak character always wore a black fedora with that black and white striped ribbon for a band.

Everything always pointed back to the fedora.

෴

The next morning, after another round of marathon typing, Josh sat in the chair rubbing the top of his head, amazed at how much bristly hair peeked out from his scalp overnight. He even thought it made him look, to put the right word to it, *manly.*

Kelsey is going to have a fit. She loves my long hair.

But that thought came far too late in the process to save Josh's skin when Kelsey finally returned.

The weather guy promised fair weather and warm temperatures. It was all the push Josh needed, and he was soon out the door and riding away from the apartment building and that damned hat. He couldn't resist riding past the place one more time, the place where that Cheap Stuff sign should be painted on a store that wasn't really there. *Too weird*, he thought again, but he kept riding down the street without pause.

He rode farther than customary and was soon winded, but he enjoyed the feeling of giving his body over to exercise. He spent far too much time lately sitting on his ass at the kitchen table vegging while he let a hat control his thoughts and fingers. He felt the air rush over his newly shaved head as he rode. It felt quite manly, truth told, and a smile started to form. Soon he was riding down the road with a wide, silly grin on his face, waving to passers-by, something he never did. Then, to his amazement, he started to sing, a rich baritone voice thrusting out in front of his bicycle. Several people walking by looked at him and smiled, enjoying the sight of a young man at peace with the world and his surroundings.

The inside truth for Josh was very different. He was trying to outrun some very odd devils: Remington and the mysterious hat. He would later admit that he had no idea of what he was about to do that day. He always hated drinking in places that masqueraded as sports bars. All it took was cold beer and a wall lined with television sets to entertain most men these days, women too, for that matter. He mostly hated it because he claimed to be the ultimate "anti-fan of sports."

But he was feeling particularly manly that day, and he considered his bike riding to be a form of sport, anyway. He locked his bike up along a fence and walked into the Salty Parrot, the Pickled Parrot, or some such name. Actually, he recalled it had a type of pickle in the name somewhere...a *firkin*... it was named the Parrot and Firkin. As his eyes adjusted to the dim interior, he walked slowly to the bar and cheeked up on the stool. When the server walked over to him he tried to look away, but was drawn to the deepest dark brown eyes he ever saw.

She smiled, "Hi, I'm Tracey, menu or just drinking?"

Josh stammered to buy time. *What do guys order? What kind of beer do I like? Why am I acting like this?*

He settled for a very cold light beer, and when she brought the mug back he said, "I...I think I will have something to eat," anything to keep her there talking to him. She looked directly into his eyes and smiled.

Did she just flirt with me? No way. Maybe she did.

"Sorry," she said with a little pout, I have a few other customers to take care of first. Take your time, I will be back." She tossed down a laminated one-page menu for him to consider before she walked to the other side of the bar to grab a bottled beer from the cooler for another patron.

Soda crackers and lollipops, he thought, one of the unusual ways he sometimes swore under his breath. *She must think I'm a total dumbass, and she's probably right.*

Josh finally placed an order for wings and fries, "and another draught, please."

Later, the other customers gradually finished their orders and faded away. It wasn't a busy time of a busy day of a busy week. "It always slows down about now," she told him. "I haven't seen you here before. Are you new in town?"

Soon they were talking and Josh told her about school, about Kelsey, and he took off his baseball cap to show off his newly-shaved head.

"Want to play trivia?" With just one other customer in the place, she pulled over two electronic handheld units and showed Josh how to answer the questions that popped up on the overhead television screen. Soon they were in a serious competition, the high score changing hands until Tracy held just a slight advantage. Josh piled up scores on history, old movies and the like. Tracy killed him with sports and current trends.

"Look at the time," she said. She looked at a man walking in who said, "Hey Trace," obviously on familiar terms with.

She turned to Josh, "This is my replacement, now I can have a beer and really whip your ass. Are you up for the challenge?"

Josh had not been drinking much, he was having too much fun and he loved talking to this pretty woman. She had a calmness about her that was the antithesis of Kelsey. Thinking of Kelsey's name gave him a moment of guilt, but he pushed that aside—a little more easily than he might have imagined. He watched Tracy walk back from the restroom, skin-tight jeans and the logo T from the sports bar.

She's perfect. That little thought turned Joshua Cody's entire world upside down. He fell in love after just a few hours in a sports bar and it hit him like a lightning bolt out of the blue. It was love almost at first sight, and he felt it more keenly than he ever felt anything in his life.

They exchanged phone numbers. Josh didn't want to leave, but the story of the young fire starter was starting to draw him back home like a magnet. Outside, she kissed him lightly on the cheek as they parted. He tried to calm himself, tried to convince himself she was only being polite. But he couldn't stop himself from singing as he rode home, singing at the top of his lungs, in fact. More than one onlooker questioned his sanity and chuckled.

He needed some caffeine for the task ahead. He opened his special stock of dark roast. It was called "Freedom's Fight," and was, of course, 'fair trade,' coffee. Things had to be very politically correct to fit in Josh's life. He savored the first taste and reached for the fedora. He was ready to type again.

chapter

NINETEEN

Two more days passed on her journey toward the mountain. For the first time during the long walk since the accident, Blaze didn't feel pain surging through her leg when she woke up. She tested her weight on the ankle, and it was tender, but not sore. The sun was well up and she cursed under her breath for not waking up sooner. She would have preferred a little darkness for a fire. She wasn't going to risk smoke, however, and chewed on a cold piece of dried meat. She stopped by a stream she crossed the night before, and after breaking her fast, knelt to wash and fill her travelling skin with water for the day ahead.

She looked around; satisfied that she hadn't left any sign of her presence, when she heard a sound, off in the distance. It was behind her to the south and east. She looked back, realizing it was a covey of birds flushed out of hiding. There was only one thing that would have caused that: the hunters were close. The circling birds gradually moved and settled back to a perch away from the disruption.

She calculated the distance; she had an hour, maybe less. An hour if they were walking. And she knew in her heart they weren't walking; they were running, which cut that hour down considerably. She stopped in a small cluster of trees for the night. They were larger trees than she was accustomed to, with white bark and leaves shimmering in the morning sunlight. The wind whispered to her through the leaves: "Listen for the rustling leaves," Stargazer told her. "They will show you the way to the mountains."

She felt an urge to run, to outdistance her pursuers. She did have one advantage, and it was a big one: She knew her destination. The pack following her could only guess and scavenge for signs of her passing. She ignored the urge to run, knowing panic to be an emotion she could ill afford.

She looked back and saw nothing. She knew they were still too far. There were hills and valleys between her and the pursuers. She guessed, correctly, they were using the low ground to avoid detection.

Turning ahead to peer through the shimmering trees, she saw a thicker grove close by. She was on the edge of a coniferous forest, though she had no name or description for it.

"When you see the pointed trees, you will know you are going in the right direction. "Look for the mountain with a crooked nose. Just to the side you will find another mountain that is shaped like dog's tail." She remembered the words clearly. "Just between those two mountains is a path that will lead you to safety, to freedom. Be warned," Stargazer held up his hand to emphasize his words, "you will be very cold walking between those two mountains, but do not stop. Do not turn back. Take the hard wood from the hills with you for your journey through the mountains."

A strong kick from the child startled her out of the reverie. It was a nudge to keep moving, to survive; for both their sakes.

Blaze found safety in the forest ahead. Amongst the thickening pines, there would be hidey holes, places of concealment. She no longer was required to outrun the hunters; she only had to outwit them.

She trotted towards the edge of the pine forest, suddenly exuberant. As she stepped out of the sunlight the forest gloom brought her a sense of welcome, a way of saying she would find refuge here.

She needed a place to hide. Just before she reached the tree line she spied one of the pursuers behind her. He was a beater, she was sure. She saw him running a zigzag course, looking at the ground for signs of her passing. She saw him getting closer to the path she had used and knew it was only a matter of time before her trail was discovered.

A few minutes into the dark of the woods, she spotted game. Their signs were everywhere, giving her confidence in finding a food supply she knew she would need for the journey ahead. When she stopped for her midday meal, she set a snare off to the side. She heard it spring on an inquisitive animal, one which would pay for its curiosity by becoming her next meal.

She took the time to gather edible plants while she bled the squirrel. To her delight, there were nuts that she knew held a valuable supply of nutrition. Once dry, she wrapped the squirrel meat carefully, burying the leavings in the ground under the low branches of a large spruce.

She moved deeper into the woods, careful to leave as little of a trail as possible. The thick carpet of pine needles would make it difficult to track her footprints in the ground. The prickly pines also resisted breakage, preferring to stab their needle-like points into her flesh. She endured the discomfort, knowing it was a small price to pay for traveling through terrain that would help to conceal her trail.

There was little sunlight filtering through to the base of the trees, but enough to make out her surroundings. Off to her right was a dark patch of leaves against the sloping ground. She stopped and looked at it carefully from a short distance and thought it covered an opening in the soil. She cautiously walked up the side of the hill and discovered a small cave. *Perfect,* she thought. She worked her way through the brush and carefully rearranged the foliage to conceal the opening from view again.

She felt safe for the first time in days, and her ankle no longer ached. She munched slowly on old dried meat and nuts, wondering about the fire she would need to cook the squirrel she had snared earlier. She smiled at the chipmunks that scurried about, providing her brief amusement. She didn't need them for food. They would all share the safety of the cave that night.

This time, she was more successful at concealing her passage than she could imagine.

The beater found a trace of her passing and pointed it out to the tracker, who spent time following her scent for as long as he could. Finally, he gave up and told the beater to go back and tell the leader that pursuit in the forest was hopeless. The beater wasn't happy to be the one to pass that message along, but he headed off at a lope to deliver the message.

The leader was livid with rage. The hunter tried to calm him down. "You know the men are good trackers. She isn't leaving any trail. This tree land tells no tales."

The leader held up his hand, showing his disdain. "It's because of Old Stargazer. He gave her these tricks. We should have cast him out before he could pass on his wisdom to the woman."

One of the beaters screwed up his courage. "We have never been so far from our clan. We need to return. The clan needs us. The girl made it this far, but it is clear she is headed into the mountains, where she is sure to find death."

The leader looked up at the mountain ridge to the north and west. He imagined her walking ahead into the cold. As angry as he was, he knew it was useless to continue. With a sigh, he accepted defeat and said, "we return to the camp at tomorrow's first light. Our group needs us."

He kept his deepest worry a secret. They no longer had a fire starter, and they nobody to show them the way with fire. Oh, the child who claimed to be the replacement for stargazer tried his best, but the leader knew he was not up to the job. He was careless with the fire bowl and his twig spinning caught flame only by sheer luck. That meant another season in the low country where food was scarce. The people were going to be hungry and he could hear the grumbling. They would question his leadership.

They aren't alone, he thought, *I don't know if I am up to the tasks ahead. Maybe they do need a new leader.*

It was a painful thought.

The next morning they decamped, following their trail back to the clan. The leader took one last look back towards the mountains, hoping for one last glimpse of her, carrying his child-to-be, the child he felt was destined to be clan leader one day.

Blaze climbed to a high tree limb and saw the hunters packing and walking away. She knew they were turning back. Instead of celebrating, she felt sad and alone.

But a tiny form was pushing its arms and legs outward, demanding to be set free from the safe confines of the womb, reminding her she would never again be truly alone. She smiled, climbed down from the tree and started back up the mountain.

chapter

TWENTY

Josh finished typing and took off the hat. He had to piss, and he couldn't put it off any longer. He watched the stream arcing towards the toilet bowl and enjoyed that sense of relief as his bladder emptied. He just finished when he heard his phone chirping. He turned to watch it vibrating and bouncing on the table top.

Without zipping, he raced to the phone and was getting ready to say hello to Kelsey when he saw it was a number he didn't know. He grinned when he realized it was the one Tracey had given him.

Hmmm, she's calling me.

He fashioned a dispassionate pose before answering. "Hello?" Not his usual "whazup?"

They talked the rest of the night. Josh kept his cell shouldered to his ear while he poured some of his special Glen Garioch into a glass. He moved to the sofa with his feet sprawled on the coffee table when his phone chirped. "Oooops. Sorry. My battery is going. I'll call you back in a few." They said good-bye and he put the phone on charge.

For Josh, bathing usually meant a quick, perfunctory shower. Tonight he treated himself to a drawn bath.

Screw it if I'm wasting good water. I deserve this.

He watched the water gradually filling up to the overflow hole and poked his toe up into the faucet, grabbing wash rag. He wiggled his toes and was just leaning back when the phone rang. He jumped out of the tub and trailed water all the way to the kitchen, large pools of beaded water fanning out on the tiled floor. He grabbed the phone and said, "Tracy..."

Then he heard Kelsey, "What? Who is Tracy?"

Josh kicked into guilty mode and tried to think of a way to cover up his enthusiasm. He knew that Kelsey had a bullshit detector and shrugged in resignation.

"I was just talking to Carson, you know, about comic books and that guy who used to talk into his wrist watch, Dick Tracey."

Kelsey was very quiet and then must have decided not to press the issue. "I'm tired Josh. Sarah and I are planning a get-together with some old friends. I won't be back as soon as I thought."

Neither of them referred to the lack of civility underlying the tone of their conversation, but it was definitely there, screaming in Josh's ear. He was decidedly prickly when he closed his phone. *Something isn't right.* He looked at the phone in his hand and scrolled down to another number. As the phone dialed, he proceeded to let out the bathwater and towel himself dry enough to pull on a pair of boxers.

"Tracey? Hi, Josh here. I'm sorry but I was taking a bath while the phone charged. Hold on a sec." He pulled a t-shirt over his head and slipped on a pair of socks. "Okay, where were we?"

They talked, Tracey invited him over, he went, and Josh later thought that shaving his head had been just the thing to give him the edge he needed. He never before made love with such passion and élan, exploring every erotic part of Tracey's body, as if he were Dr. Livingston in Africa, delving the deep, dark heart of a new and wild continent. For her part, Tracey proved to be an avid explorer of secret parts, as well. Together, they took their love making to levels each thought impossible.

They rested and loved, loved and rested, until they were both exhausted and saturated with pleasure. Josh was feeling sleepy and fought to keep his eyes open, the Morpheus of sleep calling out to him.

Then he heard Tracey say, "So, tell me about Kelsey."

Josh was between a rock and a hard place. He finally told Tracey about Kelsey, and in so doing so convinced her, and himself, that Kelsey was history. There would be a long and messy parting, with lots of screaming and accusations flying back and forth. But Josh was determined. He pledged his undying love to Tracey, and knew it was a promise he would die to keep.

It was the hat that really did it. He took the honest and forthright approach to his current situation and told Tracey about Remy, the fedora and Blaze the fire starter. Walking to his apartment he finished telling the story, she was quiet, and he feared the worst. She wouldn't believe him, about the hat and all.

Instead, she turned and said, "I want to see the hat."

He unlocked the door to his apartment and held it open for her. She stepped inside the door and stopped dead as he turned on the light. "Oh...My...God." She started to laugh, "I have never seen such a mess, ever."

Josh tried to ignore the mockery in her words and tried to divert her attention instead. "The fedora is in the kitchen," he said and waved her in like a maître d', complete with a short bow.

Tracey circled the table. "*This* is the magical fedora?" She leaned over it and her brows drew together as she stared at it, exploring it without touching it. Finally, she asked, "May I?"

He nodded.

She picked it up without an ounce of fear and commented on the heat it emitted. Without hesitation, she plopped it on her head. He waited and watched. Her eyes closed and she reached out a hand to hold the chair, to steady her from falling. Her forehead wrinkled in concentration. "I can hear words," she said with a hushed tone of reverence. "I can hear words... amazing." She took the hat off and looked at it, looking inside to examine the leather lining, rubbing the felt surface, folding and unfolding the brim. She handed it to Josh as if she were a goddess in a Greek temple handing over a chalice. "Put it on. Let me see you work."

Josh hadn't expected that. He wasn't sure he should give her a demonstration. The idea made him feel like a sideshow freak. He felt like he had something very private going with the hat. Would it be possible for him to share that? Then he looked in Tracey's eyes and knew he could share this with *her*.

He put on the fedora and let the story of Blaze, the Fire Starter, washing over him once again.

chapter

TWENTY ONE

Blaze didn't allow herself to be lulled into a false sense of well-being, even as she knew her trackers had given up. She knew how important they were to the clan. The clan existed as a unit, each person contributing their own particular talents for the survival of the clan. Each member could be assured of food, clothing and shelter. Individual members were not equipped to live apart from the clan. She knew the trackers eventually would have to return to the clan for the greater good. They were too important to the survival of the tribal unit as a whole.

She never understood the special attachment the leader had for the baby growing in her belly. He sensed the child would carry something of him into the future, something that transcended the tribe. This child would be special, and he knew it.

The old woman who spoke to the smoke had told him to take Firestarter and make her pregnant. "The child of that coupling will be special," she told him. To emphasize the power of her prediction, she gathered up and tossed the scattered bird feathers into the fire, where they curled and burned in the air, taking flight as the ashes and sparking embers rose in the heat of the fire. The leader watched them rise until they were out of sight in the night sky.

Blaze knew nothing of that prediction. She knew only that she must get past these mountains while she could still walk safely, her belly feeling taught as the skin stretched with the growing baby.

She walked up and up, until she reached the top edge of the tree line. She stopped and made a fire, without needing to hide for once. She made a large fire, a celebration of her freedom, and also necessary to keep her warm this night. It was cold and the wind was blowing down from the mountain top. She felt the moisture on the wind, dampness that would change from rain to snow as the temperature dropped. Snow was a new and startling experience for her, and she was glad that Stargazer warned her about it.

She looked in the sparse underbrush for wood that would burn to add to the fire. She watched the flames start to flicker, resisting the wind howling out of the mountain tops, and finally bursting into a full-blown blaze as the new wood caught. She started to laugh, feeling safe from pursuit for the first time in her journey. She looked up at the mountain pass, the dark clouds moving in to drape it from view like a velvety cloak of black bear fur. She had never seen snow clouds like this and was mesmerized by the huge flakes drifting down in the air in front of her.

She stoked the fire with more wood and then dragged some larger logs to the fire. She arranged them in a cross-hatched pattern and felt the heat, holding up her hands to the fire. She wrapped herself loosely in her skin blanket and slept soundly next to the fire.

She awoke on some inner cue, knowing the fire would need re-stoking during the night. She opened her eyes and thought, with a fright, the fire had gone out, but the flame was still gently flickering. The heavy snowfall blocked her sight. She looked right and left. Everything was covered in a deep layer of snow.

She jumped up and started pulling dead branches into a cross between a lean-to and a short teepee. In that near-cozy hut, she waited out a storm that dropped snow for the next day and part of the following night. Her camp remained a hollowed-out den and she was amazed that the frigid white fluff actually helped to keep her camp warm as it piled up around her.

As she munched on the dried meat she toasted over the fire, she knew she never in her life conceived of weather like this, though she listened to the warnings from Stargazer. He also told her to wait, to remain safe and warm while Nature vented its howling breath from the cold parts of the world. So, wait she did.

Finally, the storm abated and the wind turned warm again. She was puzzled by the temperature swing, but took heart from being able to see the mountain pass once again before her on the horizon.

Suddenly, a shape appeared in the corner of her vision. She jumped when she realized it wasn't human. It was a wolf, a very large wolf. Coyotes ran the desert trails, but they were easy to scare away from the camps they made. A wolf was a new experience. She didn't know enough about the creature to be afraid. It sat back on its haunches and looked at her, head cocked to the side as if puzzled. She stared back at the animal, just as curious.

She sensed the animal meant her no harm. It got up and walked around her camp in a complete circle and sat back on its haunches again, looking down at the bundle where she kept her food.

She laughed and took out a piece of dried meat and tossed it. The huge wolf caught it in mid-air and started to eat. It seemed the language of hunger was universal among the wild things of the earth. Finished with its tidbit, the animal retreated to the edge of the firelight and settled down, head resting on front paws. Then, amazingly, the beast went to sleep.

The next morning, the animal was gone. Blaze looked out at the wolf's paw prints in the snow, sadly realizing she was alone once again. Not one to linger long at a task that needed done, she took advantage of the warmth and the sunlight and started trudging through the deep snow. Only a few yards from camp, she realized her feet would freeze in the sandals. Reluctantly, she used her knife to tear of pieces of her blanket and wrapped them around her feet and ankles. The wrappings did nothing to protect the bare parts of her legs, but it would have to do. It was slow going, but she felt herself getting closer to the mountain pass with each step, and she now firmly believed she would make it to the top and over into the new world that awaited her.

As she trudged along in the snow, attention fixed upon the ground, she saw a flicker of dark among the trees and realized the wolf returned and was pacing her. It leapt through the snow, its mighty shoulders spraying snow ahead like a plow.

The wolf remained her companion to the top, and she showed her gratitude by tossing meat. The wolf didn't seem greedy, accepting the food as offered.

Finally, she reached the top. She looked back to the south and could see for what seemed like hundreds of miles. In the distance, the desert floor stretched out in an almost infinite variety of familiar earthen hues. She looked again to the north, the place where Stargazer told her to cross over the mountains. There she saw shades of green she never knew existed. As the layers of snow melted from the world, new and vibrant colors were revealed.

She turned, expecting the wolf to follow. She looked all around, but there was no sign of the animal. On the far side of the pass, she made camp for another long night when she reached the outskirts of the tree line. That night, as she stirred the fiery embers, she could hear a mournful howling. She didn't know why, but began to cry—a long mournful wail, echoing the sound of the wolf that remained behind. Once again, she longed for companionship. Stifling her tears, she reminded herself that she wasn't alone; the child was ever with her. There was a long way to go, and she didn't know where her trail would end.

But, she trusted Stargazer. She looked heavenward in the clearing night sky. There he was, winking down at her, ever vigilant.

chapter

TWENTY TWO

"This is beautiful. It's remarkable and beautiful," Tracey said. She said those words with a hushed awe. Josh breathed a deep sigh, finally able to share this with someone other than a screaming redhead who thought he was crazy and selfish.

"I don't know where the story comes from, and it frightens me and intrigues me at the same time," he said.

"You have no idea?" she asked.

"None, I tell you. As soon as I take the hat off, the words stop coming to me. I'm not as frightened as I was at the beginning, but I don't think I could admit this to anyone else. Kelsey couldn't handle it," and was sorry for bringing her into the conversation.

But Tracey understood and didn't object. She was self-assured and untroubled by the mention of Kelsey's name.

"I think you have to be very careful with this," she said thoughtfully. "Do you have anyone who might be able to explain any of this?"

He shrugged. "I wish I did."

He told her in detail how he found Remington and the fedora. She went with him back to the location, but it didn't help. He was no closer to understanding that strange store than before. They looked for over an hour, to no avail.

Tracey worked as a server at a bar and was unsophisticated in an academic sense. She finished eleventh grade, but events in her life conspired to prevent her from going any further. What made her special was that she was unimpressed with Josh's big brain. She knew he was brilliant, but she also knew that all that knowledge bouncing around in his head caused him to lose focus from time to time. What good did all those smarts do then?

But Josh knew she was smart—the kind of smart that he respected. She helped ground him, and at the same time, she found a way that encouraged him to stretch.

No matter how well matched their talents were, neither could dream up any explanation for the strange story about people in a place and time that didn't exist. Or did it?

They walked the streets, enjoying the evening and talking non-stop. They turned ideas inside and out. She suggested a stop at a store that specialized in science fiction. They talked to the owner and hinted at the story. The owner could give them no clues.

The next morning, they ate breakfast and went to the university library. They scoured books that speculated on the tribal customs and wandering patterns of prehistoric nomadic peoples. They took notes on what was known and what was guessed about such people. They were able to put some of the puzzle together, but there were large gaps—holes of information that prevented them from fully understanding Blaze and her story.

Josh tried calling the expert again, but as soon as he started to talk about the story, the man slammed down the phone after growling out, "Don't call me again!" Josh was sure the man added "ass..." to the end of that request.

Josh and Tracey headed back to the apartment. As they walked, Josh slipped his hand around hers and felt as though he were taking possession, not of her, but of a feeling inside himself. He owned a new feeling of love and commitment. It was something that he never felt with Kelsey.

He had an epiphany and stopped.

"What is it?" Tracey asked, and the question was reflected in her eyes, as well.

"I love you, Tracey," he said, and started to laugh. What he didn't do was share the revelation: He suddenly *knew* they were destined to tell and publish the strange story of Blaze the Firestarter.

He was about to propose marriage, of all things, when he saw Kelsey storming down the sidewalk. He swore he could see steam sprouting from her head.

"Well, there goes a perfect day," he muttered, squaring his shoulders in preparation for the onslaught coming his way.

Kelsey was a drama queen, in case you haven't figured that out. Today, she was at the top of her game. She wanted to hurt Josh. She already endured his self-absorbed behavior just long enough, and then *BAM!* Along came that damned hat. She picked it up, intending to throw it down the trash chute. But when she grabbed at it, the evil thing was so hot her fingers started to burn, and she dropped it to the floor. She backed away suddenly, absolutely terrified of the fedora.

She backed away from the fedora a few feet when she realized there was the presence of another woman inside the apartment. Kelsey's territorial instincts flew into high gear, even though she intended to leave Josh. She returned home from her weekend determined to dump the big-brained, nerdy geek. She *would* get her revenge for all the perceived wrongs she blamed on him.

She slammed the door of the apartment on the way out and heard something crash to the floor and break. *I hope it's that damned typewriter,* though she knew it wasn't.

Then, to top off her day, as she walked around the corner, there was Josh—holding another woman's hand.

"Sonofabitch!" Kelsey yelled and stormed towards them.

It could have been an ugly scene if it weren't for Tracey outwitting and outmaneuvering the fiery redhead. She moved up and put her arms around Kelsey, embracing her and calling her by name, as though she were a long-lost friend. It was so disarming that Kelsey just stopped in mid rage. She broke free of the other woman's grasp and stepped back, looking completely and utterly baffled. Without another word, she turned and stalked off. She never even looked back. Later, she sent some friends over to get her stuff. They acted a bit sheepish about their assignment, liking Josh as well—almost more than they liked Kelsey, truth be told.

One of the guys, Bryan, whispered to Josh as he was leaving, "I totally get why you made the switch, dude," and gave Josh a high five. Josh just smiled and put his arm around Tracey as the guys walked out the door with Kelsey's stuff.

Later that night, Josh and Tracey curled up with some popcorn and an old movie. "You have to see this," Josh said. "Joel McCrea is a foreign correspondent, and check out the hat he wears," but Tracey was more interested in the hat that Greta Garbo was wearing.

"Let's not put on the hat tonight," she whispered when the movie was over. Their lovemaking was all-consuming that night. Remington and the fedora would have to wait for morning.

chapter

TWENTY THREE

This side of the mountain felt different. She felt it immediately. There was warmth to the wind as she descended the far side of the mountain. The trees were different, not the acutely pointing pines trying to prick the sky to bleeding. These were trees with wide, smooth limbs and broad leaves that rustled as the wind rippled past. She was unsure of the wood, now, not knowing which kinds to choose for the different types of fires she would need. Would they burn with smoke? Would they burn too hot for the food? Did they have to be dried first? The technical questions raced through her head.

She wasn't sure when it first started, but she suddenly felt very dizzy, lightheaded. Then, as she blinked, her world started to turn and she was falling back, the bright sunlit sky fading into black as she fainted and fell. She thought she heard the voice of the leader calling her back. She heard the cackling of the other women when they found out she was with child, resenting her because they knew it was the leader's child, one to be favored above all.

She heard the footsteps of the trackers and the beaters.

Then she heard the mournful howling, the sound of her strange wolf from a faraway place. She tried to make sense of it all as the sounds competed for her attention inside her swirling head. She heard the words of Stargazer, almost as though he crouched next to her, whispering in the night. "It will be all right, child. You are safe now. Rise, walk, and look to the future."

As the blue sky came back into focus, the dizziness passed. She started to laugh and was suddenly ravenous. She started to tear pieces of dried meat away from the bones with her teeth, devouring the remainder of her carefully stored pine nuts, trying to quench her appetite.

She also now sensed the child growing in her was going to be a male child, and he would have a special destiny. She was only slightly disappointed the child would not be a daughter she wanted to pass on her secrets to.

Man and nature couldn't defeat her, now. She bested them both. She had only to protect herself from her own doubts and misgivings. She had to keep going. There was a place waiting for her and her son. It wasn't far, now.

She rubbed her engorged stomach and knew it wouldn't be long before the birthing time was upon her. She got up from the ground and found a walking stick. It was a sturdy walking stick, something she could use for balance. It would also serve well as a weapon if needed.

She had no idea who, if anyone, lived on this side of the mountain. She had no idea of the animals she might encounter here, if they were dangerous or not. She saw waves of rain in the distance, like grey brush strokes against dark clouds. They were benign, she thought. The sun broke through again, and she saw it as a beacon, calling her home, and she continued her journey down the mountain.

The grass was tall; she could barely see over the top. She saw a deer. It was a magnificent male with antlers, tossing its head and then ambling off, unafraid of her presence in his world.

Before her was an open field, small animals scurrying about in the sunshine. Here was an abundance of food she had never known in her whole life. She would only take what was needed to stay alive, however, leaving the rest undisturbed.

Birds circled her high above like a halo—flocks of birds, adorned in brightly colored plumage. They were nothing like the drab colors of the desert birds, the hawks and vultures that scoured the desert floor. Her son would see a wondrous world, full of new and exciting sights and sounds.

As Blaze was celebrating her amazing new life, she heard an odd sound. It was like the sound the deer made as they ran, yet different—more thunderous—not the hushed hoof beats of the lithe and graceful animals she was used to. A rhythmic clopping sound floated on the air, steadily growing louder. Out of the copse of trees, a horse—as yet unknown to her as a horse—was charging towards her. She let out a scream. She had never seen a beast such as this. It was huge, white with mottled shades of grey over its body.

The horse ran straight at her, and she was too terrified to move, standing directly in its path, transfixed. She put up her hands as though she could stop the creature, trying to stifle her screams. What terrified her even more was the man astride the horse. He wore animal skins over his entire body and a hat of some kind atop his head. He pulled the horse to a stop, only inches in front of her and looked down, assessing his new find. He looked neither friendly nor unfriendly. His was a look of simple inquisitiveness. He stared at her for a long time and then spoke in a guttural language that made no sense to Blaze.

She held up her arms for protection as he dismounted and walked over to her. He reached out and touched her and she flinched in response. Her body trembled and she averted her gaze from the man. Although she knew other clans existed in the world, her mind was unprepared to meet another human being. The leader and the wise ones of her clan always dealt with other tribes.

Finally, he reached around her waist and with powerful hands, lifted her up and placed her sideways on the horse, motioning her to stay put. Then he picked up her belonging and handed them up to her. He led the horse to the north and east, talking in a language Blaze couldn't comprehend. She tried to speak back in her own language, to tell him of her purpose in this land, but he only turned and looked at her, not comprehending. The horse loped along, easily carrying his burden. At first, Blaze had a difficult time maintaining her position on the giant beast. Her concentration was fixed upon maintaining her seat, even at this easy pace. The man whistled and a white dog sprinted out of the woods. It looked just like her friend the wolf, only smaller.

Blaze had no experience with animals that could be ridden. She only knew walking or running. Despite her initial fear and the difficulty of staying on top of the creature, she found she liked riding this thing; she liked it a lot, in fact. As they passed over the field at a lazy pace, she smiled and grew braver with ability to remain atop the horse and let go of the mane with one hand. As her body relaxed from its initial fear response, she learned to let her body flow into the rhythm of the horse's gait, making the creature easier to ride. She drew one arm over her belly, rubbing the spot where the child kicked most frequently, and started to hum a quiet song that matched the rocking gait of the horse.

chapter

TWENTY FOUR

Josh took extra care with breakfast that morning. He left Tracey curled up in bed, knees drawn to her chest, her arms wrapped around two pillows. It looked like she was trying to squeeze the life out of them. It was her snoring that awoke him. On the intake, he could hear the air rushing through her nose in a high-pitch whistle. Then, she emitted a deep, nasal moan— half honking, half jet airliner revving for take-off.

He wanted to be irritated, but it sounded too funny. He was half tempted to grab a tape recorder. He roused himself, splashed cold water on his face and stumbled into the kitchen still a tad groggy. He reached past the everyday coffee and pulled out his special brew. He poured the beans into the grinder and savored the scent the beans released as the blade whirred around, reducing them to a fine Turkish grind. He silently counted: one thousand and one; one thousand and two; one thousand and three...until he reached one thousand and ten. He was precise with this ritual, especially so with his expensive special blend. The finer the grind, the darker and richer the coffee it ultimately produced.

You already know Josh prides himself on being cheap, though he prefers the word "thrifty." One of the few exceptions he allowed himself (beyond the outrageously expensive single-malt scotch) was the $19.45 per pound, fair trade, handpicked coffee beans he's currently grinding for precisely ten seconds. Whenever he breaks out the expensive stuff, he imagines the revolutionary salutes of the bean pickers, swinging their arms in unison as they march from their barracks to the coffee bean fields, shouting revolutionary slogans in Spanish (as well as a few anti-American ones) and singing some Julio Iglesias song as they worked. Josh admits he's not sure if dear old Julio is as well loved in Central and South America as he is in the North. Regardless, it is an image that always makes him smile.

But the *real* reason he spends so much for the coffee is because it's *so damned good.*

The toaster popped up the last of the bagels. He spread cream cheese, adding a little extra for the occasion. He put them on plates and put the plates on a tray he managed to dig up in the back of one of the kitchen cabinets. He poured two small glasses of orange juice and set them on the tray next to the coffee cups. They were souvenir cups from Niagara Falls (well, that wasn't entirely accurate); he swiped them from a restaurant there. Still, he always considered them reminders of a nice weekend he once had there. *What was the name of that girl*

I went with? It was the one before Kelsey. He pushed that thought quickly aside as he looked through the door at Tracey and felt a trace, no pun intended, of guilt.

There was a vase on the kitchen counter with five wilted flowers, long past their promise of beauty. *What the hell,* he thought, as he picked the best one out of the array and put in alongside the plate with the bagel he toasted for Tracey.

He whistled as he walked in with the tray and watched her uncurl, stretching like a lazy cat, rubbing her eyes.

"Ohhhhhhh, sweet," she moaned, drawing out the ohhhh far longer than required. She grabbed the pillows and slid them behind her back and squinched up along the bed until she was sitting, propped up against the now pillowed headboard. She made a table with her lap and Josh placed the tray down with a flourish befitting a snooty matre d'.

"I've been thinking," Tracey said after she took a small sip of orange juice. She waited for Josh to respond. When he didn't, she went on. "What do you think would happen if *I* tried to wear the hat and type?" She immediately noticed that he was uncomfortable with the idea, but he didn't want to hurt her feelings. "It was just an idea," she shrugged, "but I was wondering."

"You heard some words when you put the hat on, didn't you?" he finally asked, taking his time.

"I heard words, sort of, but not complete sentences. They were disconnected, disjointed, and not really belonging to a voice, per se. I want to put the hat on again and just see what happens. Can I? Pleeease?" she said, pleading with her eyes as well as her lips.

He didn't decide right away, but finished breakfast instead. He was pleased when she told him how good the coffee was. Everything about her seemed to validate him in some way. With Kelsey, there had always been the friction of competition between them. When he said hot, she would say cold. Tracey stood up for her uniqueness, but they didn't need confrontation in order to come to a mutually beneficial agreement, or even to agree to disagree. They talked, exchanged ideas, and listened to each other. How different this was from his relationship with Kelsey. Tracey had a way of taking his guard down.

When they finished breakfast, he carried the tray and dishes out to the kitchen and came back carrying the fedora. It was almost as if he were making a formal introduction, even though she had touched and worn the hat before. She took it with a twinkle of delight in her eye and placed it on her head. She closed her eyes for a moment in concentration and then a smile started to spread over her face.

"I *hear* something...women talking, I think. They are excited and talking about—"

"Don't talk, stop!" Josh held up his hand. "Take off the hat."

She reluctantly took the hat off with a frown and placed it on her knees, drawn up to her chest. She looked like a chastised toddler in that moment and Josh's heart went out to her.

"It may be an important part of the story," he said more gently. "Can you type?"

"Not very fast," she admitted.

He took the hat in one hand and pulled her out of bed with the other, leading her out to the kitchen. He pulled out the chair and had her sit in front of Remy.

She looked at it and then up at Josh. "I have never seen one of these before I met you. I don't know how to use it." He was very patient and showed her how to insert the paper. He showed her how to push down on the keys and how they would fly up to strike the ribbon and produce words on the blank paper. He urged her to simply practice, without the hat, and knew to leave her alone while she struggled with the learning curve.

He pushed a DVD into the slot and settled back to watch an old movie. He had chosen one of his favorites, a film noir in black and white movie with Orson Welles and Charlton Heston. He had seen this movie so often; he began unconsciously mouthing the dialogue as the actors played out their roles. He picked up the remote and pushed the pause button. He watched a rotund Orson Welles in freeze frame, his evil persona emphasized by the dark shadows and indirect lighting. The movie was pretty corny and overly dramatic, he admitted there was just something about it that drew him.

He put the remote on the coffee table and walked into the kitchen. Tracey was hunched over the keyboard and muttering something. He heard her say, "Remington," but it wasn't said kindly. He saw the tension in her shoulders and reached down to softly massage her back and neck. He felt her respond, her muscles relaxing to his touch.

"You must be more than ready for a break?"

She nodded with relief, stood up and stretched. They decided to head out for a walk, basking in the sun's warmth. They looked in store windows and watched people as they passed by, laughing at one toddler trying to climb up on a bench, a look of utter determination on his face, little pink tongue poking out the corner of his mouth while his mother urged him on.

"I've been thinking about it," Josh finally said. "This whole thing with the hat has been wearing me down, and I'm waking up tired. My studies are suffering. If the hat talks to you like it does to me, collaboration will make half the work for each of us."

Tracey smiled as though her fondest wish had just been granted. "Let's give it a try," she said with genuine enthusiasm, and they started to walk faster, almost running back home. Josh wasn't quite sure just when his apartment had also become hers. It had been, what, a couple days? He shook his head and laughed the thought away as they raced the last block back.

When they got to the apartment, they were out of breath and laughing. Josh never felt so alive, never felt such a sense of sharing.

It was an almost solemn occasion as she sat down in front of Remy, muttering his formal name, Remington. She slid the carriage back and forth, listening to the bell ringing at the end of a slide. She flexed her fingers, imitating a concert pianist, preparing to play a Chopin etude.

"The hat, sir."

Placing it on her head, she frowned in concentration, listening to the excited voices of the women sliding through her head like oil. The conversation was *greasy*, difficult to grasp and hang on to. Her forehead squeezed into tight wrinkles of determination. After a moment, she nodded to herself, lifted her hands and her fingers started *tap, tap, tapping* the keyboard, slowly at first, and then picking up speed. She told Josh later that night that she didn't even have to think about typing, her fingers did the work without any conscious effort on her part, stopping only to remove a page filled with words and inserting a clean sheet. "The hat told me the story." She shook her head in awed disbelief.

But that was later. For the moment, she simply listened to the voices of the story as the hat unfolded the tale through her fingers.

chapter

TWENTY FIVE

Blaze rocked to the gait of the horse and looked around at the vivid green life passing by. Coming from the desert side of the mountain, she had never seen such a lush setting. The man kept turning his head back and saying something. The words were just sounds to her, but she sensed that he was a man she could trust. He hadn't hurt her and he didn't seem to be speaking to her harshly. All in all, those were definitely good signs of his character and intent.

At a stream, he stopped and motioned for her to stay seated on the horse. He took an animal skin container and scooped up cold water and lifted it up to her. As she tilted her head back to drink, he continued to speak in his strange language, but she heard the softness of his words. He reached up and patted her stomach and grinned, nodding his head and tilting his head back until he was laughing loudly, a sound of joy and celebration.

She opened a pouch and took out some of her own dried meat. She held it up and he nodded. He helped her down and she quickly gathered wood and within moments started a fire. He looked at her, admiring the skill with which she performed the task that was second nature to her.

They heated the dried meat, dousing it with a little water from the stream to soften it and washed it down with water he gathered in the skin. When they finished, he lifted her back on the horse, his concern for a mother-in-waiting touched her. It was unlike the harsh nature of the desert men she lived with all her life. For them, life was harsh and only the strongest survived. They did not offer any quarter to the clan members, regardless of age. Though they knew procreation was necessary to the life of the clan, a child unable to survive the meanness of the desert was a liability; even if they were still in the womb. She wondered at the difference, but could draw no conclusions.

By mid-afternoon, the sun was beginning its downward path against the sky. They came out of a thick forest, following a trail that appeared to be the result of constant footsteps over a long period of time. Because she came from a nomadic background, her people were constantly moving in search of game and plants. They seldom walked the same way twice: there were no trails.

She looked down and wasn't sure what it all meant, but she knew this was significant somehow. This was different place, and she started to guess there were different rules for survival here. She knew she would have to rethink the lessons she learned, what she was taught all her life.

As they crested a hill, her jaw dropped. She never before saw a village and was unprepared for the grouping of thatched huts. At first, she wondered how they managed to pack up these enormous structures and carry them around following their source of food. She quickly realized these people didn't move at all; the abundance of life and food here made it completely unnecessary. It was a permanence that was both intriguing and frightening. Her life to this point consisted of only transitory concepts; the idea of *permanence* was beyond her ability to imagine.

She saw a group of women clustered together in the center of the huts, a clearing that held large racks lined with animal skins drying by a large, central fire. They were laughing and working side-by-side, and when one looked up and saw her emerging through the trees, the woman shrieked and pointed, babbling to her companions loudly. They all looked up and came running, their eyes wide with astonishment at the strange-looking woman sitting sideways on the horse. Curious villagers emerged from their huts, but remained stock still as Blaze and the man were surrounded by the group of fearless females.

It was obvious they were asking the man a multitude of questions and he was patiently nodding his head and answering. The women looked up at Blaze, some with smiles, knowing it wouldn't be long before her baby was born.

The women in the compound were well-fed, more round in appearance than those of her old clan. They tied their hair back and had bright eyes. By contrast, Blaze, a desert woman, looked like a wild thing from the forest, hair tangled, face smeared by dirt from her days of travel and having never known a bath due to a lack of water in the desert. Looking at these women, she couldn't help it; she started to cry. Blaze didn't know where she was, and she had no idea who these people were, nor could she understand a word of what they were saying. Soon, her crying turned to a wracking, heart-wrenching moan.

Alarmed, the huge man lifted her down from the horse and simply stood there, not knowing how to comfort her or why she was upset. He was roughly pushed away by the women, who *tsked* him and shooed him off to the side, shielding their new prize from his man eyes.

One by one, they surrounded her to comfort her and hold her tight. They didn't talk; they simply cooed and held her and stroked her arms. One brushed Blaze's hair back and another mysteriously produced a moist cloth and gently started to wash the tear-streaked grime away from her face. All the feelings of loneliness and fear and worry left her as on the wings of a bird, carried into the sky.

She miraculously and instantly felt accepted into a sisterhood of grace that transcended language and origin. They gently herded her toward the village, prattling in their strange language. As they walked, the first contraction pain took her and she stopped suddenly with the unfamiliar pain and tightness. The women stroked her hair and arms and back, gently prodding her on toward the huts as the cramping eased and she could walk again. They smiled at her knowingly, as her eyes filled with apprehension and fear. These women knew the signs and were wise in the ways of birth and labor. They were not surprised to see Blaze starting the labor process so soon after her long journey.

By this time, the men from the surrounding fields heard the commotion and started drifting in one by one. They stood in a ring on the immediate edge of the camp and watched the women comfort the newcomer. Even the men were intimately familiar with the mysteries of birth and death, and they knew they were watching the miracle of a new life coming into the world.

One woman stood up and took charge. No one quarreled or contradicted her. She led Blaze by the hand across the center of the village into a dark tent. Another woman rolled out a woven mat and Blaze carefully eased herself down to lie upon it. Someone placed a skin beneath her head as another was stretched over her to keep her warm. Outside, Blaze could see men doing the unthinkable: they were taking over the women's chores while the women were busy attending to Blaze's needs. She could hear women's voices raised in excitement as water boiled in large clay pots that Blaze had never seen before. She watched the woman nearest her unfold a large piece of cloth and begin to tear it in smaller pieces prepared for the time ahead. Cloth was also unknown to her, as the desert nomadic clans had not yet developed looms for weaving. Despite the intermittent contractions, Blaze was fascinated by the material and longed to touch a piece to see what it felt like. Too soon, however, the strength of her contractions drew her attention to the business at hand and the comings and goings around her turned into a haze of pain that burned into the coming night.

The baby didn't arrive until the next morning as the sun's first rays peeked above the horizon, but Blaze was comforted throughout the night by the women around her. She was never left alone; someone was always beside her, soothing her forehead with a cooling cloth and speaking softly in the words of a strange language. She found she didn't need to know the precise translation of the words to understand their meaning.

Blaze later thought about the incredible pain of that experience, but it was a pain that quickly faded with the first sound of a lusty cry. Her baby announced his arrival. No one who was there that morning could even guess the part this child would play in their own futures.

Blaze wept as the midwife gently cleaned and lifted the squalling child for her to hold.

On the far side of the mountain, in the desert, an old crone dropped the ritual feathers into a small fire and chanted. She turned to the leader and told him his son was born. The leader stood and walked to the edge of the camp and looked up at the mountain pass, knowing he could never cross it to find the child. As he stood there watching the darkening sky, his eyes were drawn to a meteor streaking across the northern sky, flickering flames trailing behind. He knew it was a sign, one no longer meant for his clan.

chapter

TWENTY SIX

Tracey never experienced exhaustion like this. In all of her years carrying trays of food and slinging drafts of beer across the bar, she often felt the bone-aching tired from physical labor. This was different; it was a mental fatigue that drew her shoulders forward into a slouch and bowed her head with the weight of the words and ideas flowing through her head. She took off the fedora, set it wearily on the table next to Remington and immediately felt the muscles in her arms and shoulders relax.

She realized she was so caught up in the story, she hadn't realized the strength it sapped from her body, the energy needed for her fingers to transmit the story through the mechanical arms of the typewriter onto the paper.

She looked at the hat and smiled. Josh inserted a small card into the nylon band, it said, "Warning: Novelist at Work, Beware." It was meant to warn visitors that they might be written into the story.

Not this story, though, she knew. This was a story from a long ago time, before history was recorded, even before history was a legend passed from one generation to the next through stories and folk tales.

For some unknown reason, Tracey began to cry, the responsibility for telling this story crashing against her like a tsunami. She sensed it would be a wave that, once deposited onto the shores of the blank white paper, would recede, leaving debris and sorrow in piles. The story was so real to her, so believable, that she knew it was true. An awful reality haunted her: to others, the story would sound so *un*believable that anyone reading it would think it was merely the wild imagination of two young, wine-addled wannabe writers and dismiss it as mere fiction. But it was more than fiction for the story's creators.

She walked into the other room, practically dragging her feet. Josh had fallen asleep and the old black and white movie was playing, the sound muted. She plopped down next to him on the couch and gently shook him. "We need to talk."

Josh came slowly awake, rubbing his eyes, "Huh?"

"Josh, the story is so beautiful and so sad," Tracey said softly. She glanced at the hat lying on the table. "The words stop coming when I take off the hat. Is that the way it was for you?"

Josh thought about what she said before he responded. "The story is sad sometimes, yes. But mostly, I just want to know the story, what comes next. I want the story to continue and never end. It's hard to take the hat off sometimes; the words stop flowing and I feel sort of empty when they're gone."

"Did you ever wonder what would have happened to the story if you never found Remington and that fedora?"

She gave voice to a thought that had been creeping around his own mind like a cat circling its prey. He hadn't wanted to voice it, even to himself, but, Tracey opened the door and he couldn't close it now. "Maybe," he said, "but I guess the point is moot. I found them, and now I just have to know. Don't you?"

"More than anything," she answered.

Tracey jumped up and turned up the lights. "Come on, Josh," she encouraged, waving her arms. "We need to do something, *anything* but put that damned hat on." She looked at the hat with a touch of guilt.

The apartment was a total mess. Josh wasn't what you would call a tidy person; in fact, he was sometimes proud of his tolerance for clothes and things strewn about. The chaos he saw as he looked around the place was a mirror of the chaos of unordered thoughts flashing around in his head most of the time. Kelsey was a neat freak, and their two opposing natures often led to bitter shouting and defensive sulking; Kelsey shouting and Josh defending.

Tracey seemed to be more tolerant of his disorder, but she had her limits, and they had been reached. With gentle prodding and a large dollop of humor, she soon had Josh on his hands and knees cleaning and scrubbing. They started in the living room, sorting through the disorder and sorting through piles of clothes, DVD cases, text books and the like, arranging them into something resembling order.

The kitchen was the hardest, with an array of food-stained plates and pots from one end of the kitchen counter to the other, stuck in gooey piles. They cleaned with the radio volume jacked up high enough the neighbors pounded on the common wall. They looked at each other and laughed but turned the sound down and finished the kitchen clean-up.

The one part of the apartment they didn't disturb was the table; Remy sat patiently next to a growing pile of manuscript pages turned upside down. Two boxes of typing paper lay close by. Tracey picked up the fedora and placed it at a rakish angle on the carriage, wondering with an ironic grin if the words could just go directly to the pages without the need for a human conduit. No such luck.

When they finished with the kitchen, they targeted the bathroom until the sink, tub and other porcelain fixtures were sparkling. Josh stripped down, jumped in the tub and started scrubbing down the tile walls. Tracey slipped out of her shorts and drew the t-shirt up over her head and stripped away her bra and panties and soon they were engaged in an activity that had nothing to do with cleaning. Afterwards, they showered and managed to find clean clothes in the bedroom.

"I feel like Chinese," Josh said and pulled out a drawer, rummaging around until he found a menu. He over-ordered so they could have cold leftovers to enjoy. When the meal was delivered, he opened a bottle of wine.

The empty Chinese food containers laid a new foundation for disorder in the kitchen, and empty plates and chopsticks laid discarded on the coffee table in the living room. Their cleanliness vow certainly did not last long. Instead of cleaning again, they made love on the sofa, then the floor. It started out laughing and joyful, rolling and twisting, but turned serious and loving before it ended.

Tracey stood up and walked to the bedroom door. "I'm beat. I *have* to get some sleep," she mumbled in a dreamy tone that matched the wistful look in her eyes.

Josh didn't move, but remained on the floor and gazed up at the ceiling, noticing vague shapes in the speckled paint, the way kids notice shapes in the summer clouds. They were shapes he never noticed before, never having been on his back, on the floor, in this position before.

It was a long time before he slipped into a pair of jeans and found his t-shirt draped over an end-table lamp. He smiled and remembered flinging it there in his moment of passionate undressing.

He couldn't sleep though. He brewed some of his special coffee. He had to find out. He had to know where the story would go next. He picked up the fedora and welcomed the warmth he felt to the touch. He sipped his coffee and savored the rich, dark roast. He knew when he put the hat on he would be too busy to enjoy the luxury of coffee. Once he drained the cup, he set it on the table next to the manuscript and picked up the hat, ready to continue the work.

chapter

TWENTY SEVEN

Blaze didn't know why, but she knew she was safe with these people. She felt the caring in the gentle touch of the women. They conveyed their understanding, knowing the pain and joy that childbirth brought.

She could see the concern in the eyes of the men, gathered behind in the edges of the light. She saw the giant standing among them, the one who placed her on his horse. She sensed that he somehow saved her life. While she was certainly grateful for that, her deepest gratitude was really for the fact he saved the life of her son, lying on her stomach, his head between her breasts. He was still yelling at the top of his lungs, as if to announce his arrival, letting everyone know he was special.

Blaze knew from his very first breath that she would lay down her life for this baby. Voices were swarming through her head, whispering that he was special, born to a great destiny.

Gradually, a sense of well-being flowed over Blaze and her eyes started to close, but she forced them open again. A broad smile swathed her face. The old woman who took charge stood, looking around, speaking in a strange language that Blaze could not understand, waving and shooing everyone out through the door. She returned and knelt. She reached for a woven blanket and covered Blaze and the baby and squatted next to the two of them. Blaze closed her eyes and slept a deep and dreamless sleep. It was the first real sleep she enjoyed in a long, long time.

As she drifted to sleep she heard the voice of Stargazer, but couldn't make out a meaning. She felt an urge to start running at the sound of the Leader's voice. *It's a dream...*and she was asleep.

The next sound she heard was a sound she had no description for: It was the sound of a rooster crowing. Nothing in her experience gave her a comparison for that startling screech. Blaze opened her eyes at once, the weight of her baby absent from her chest. She stifled a scream when the old woman put a reassuring hand on the new mother's shoulder. She pointed to the side where a young woman looked proud to have been chosen to be wet-nurse to the stranger's baby.

Blaze watched her son suckling hungrily, his mouth grasping the breast around the nipple and making loud sucking noises. The sight and sound reassured Blaze, and she knew she needed more rest for the job of motherhood that awaited her when she recovered.

Another woman entered the hut carrying a wooden bowl. She showed Blaze how to tip the bowl and sip the contents. It was a smooth, milky texture with a strange aroma. Blaze was tentative, but her ravenous hunger took control and she tilted the bowl until the food was gone. She was used to dried meat and berries and some foraged grain, but this was a new experience for her. The new woman reached into the fold of her clothes and drew out something hard on the outside and soft on the inside and handed it to Blaze, motioning her to eat it. Later, Blaze would know it as bread. It was much different from the flatbread her clan made from the bits of grain they sometimes found at the edges of the desert. She thought the new food tasted odd and hoped they still had her supply of dried game. The meal proved to be far more filling than expected. Blaze gathered enough energy to ignore the pain in her stomach and between her legs and began to sit up. The old woman rushed to help and laughed when Blaze waved away her help and pointed to the baby.

The nursemaid handed the boy back and Blaze felt the milk in her breasts stirring painfully. She was ready, and with bliss she couldn't explain, she felt her son taking nourishment from her breast releasing the ache inside her.

The women knew a great deal about giving birth and they knew it would not be good for Blaze to become idle. They encouraged her to start moving, to sit up and to stand. Each day saw a marked increase in Blaze's energy. She was able to sit and stand, holding her son and gently caressing his brow and head.

Finally, after only seven days, the other woman pointed to the door. She stepped out and was greeted by a brilliant sun, just past the high time of the day. She looked around in amazement at the arrangement of huts. They were constructed out of a grassy material, thatched on the sides and top. Blaze had never seen such permanence before, and she didn't know how to interpret it all.

On first look there didn't seem to be much activity. Everyone stopped work at the sight of the new mother and baby. Blaze could hear excited voices drifting on the wind currents. Then they all started back to work. Men were walking in a field between long, straight rows of green plants. The men would bend over from time to time, straighten up and stoop again, walking down the rows as they worked. One man carried a large container of leaves gathered from the plants. When it was full, he carried it to a large, flat surface where women sat, pulling the leaves apart and handing pieces to other women who were pounding them to a pulp. Other women were standing by racks made of limbs from trees. Animal skins were draped over the frames, drying in the sun.

She saw other men, farther out from the village, walking horses loaded with large parcels. Blaze turned back to look at the camp itself. In the very center of the huts was a huge fire. At last, Blaze saw something she recognized and started to smile.

Two small children rushed up to her and tugged on her wrap. They had the excited look so easy for children. They were laughing and pointing at the baby. On instinct, Blaze squatted slowly with only a slight wince and held out the baby for their inspection. One of the children, a girl, pulled the wrap from the baby and laughed, saying something as she pointed at the penis. That was the start for Blaze. Now she understood the word they used to describe boy child, one with a penis. She rolled the word around in her head, memorizing it. She turned to a woman nearby and said the word. The woman nodded and Blaze took her first step in learning her new language.

chapter

TWENTY EIGHT

It was late when Josh finished this latest part of the story. Just as he thought he caught a glimpse of the direction this remarkable story was taking, he became uneasy. It was related to the questions raised earlier by Tracey: Who would believe it? How could such a story come from a hat?

He knew with certainty he would never mention that fact to anyone else. Scholars would no doubt disbelieve the details. How could anyone know what life was like before history, anyway? Besides, Josh was no longer sure *where* the story came from really mattered anymore. It was simply a story he and Tracey were putting down on paper together.

While he was typing, he ignored his cell vibrating on the table. He wouldn't allow any interruptions in the story flow. It rang for a second time and he put it on the kitchen counter, out of his reach.

Taking a break, he stood up, stretched and poured some more coffee. He wasn't worried that the caffeine would keep him awake. Sipping his coffee, he reached and picked up the phone. A flashing light indicated waiting messages. There were three voice mails and two text messages.

He sipped his coffee from a mug in his left hand and flipped the phone cover with his right, a casual, practiced maneuver. He thumbed the keys and listened to the voice mail first. Two were from Kelsey, she wanted to talk. She missed him. She loved him. She sounded desperate.

The third call was from his faculty advisor. "You haven't been to class for two weeks now and you are seriously behind. You need to call me, now." It was the chilling emphasis of the word *now* that caught Josh's attention.

He looked at the calendar and the take-out containers littering the kitchen and realized he and Tracey had barely left the apartment in over two weeks. She called the sports bar where she worked and told them to "stuff it." Josh was so engrossed with Remington and the story he hadn't bothered with classes, papers or even a courtesy call to say, "Sorry I'm tied up at the moment and can't get away for classes." He laughed at that thought. He and Tracey experimented with bondage the night before and he had literally been tied up.

He read the two text messages. The words were different, but the message was the same in both. Kelsey said she made a mistake and now wanted to reconcile with Josh. "Plz, plz, pleeeease," she pleaded.

Pathetic, Josh thought and deleted all the voice mail and text messages. *The heck with school,* he told himself as he turned off the phone.

He needed to piss and walked into the bathroom. Looking in the medicine cabinet mirror he was shocked. *Who is that man in the mirror?* It had been days since he shaved, and while his beard didn't grow at a particularly fast rate, it was looking rather raggedy.

His eyes were seriously bloodshot and his hair beyond unruly, qualifying for truly awful. His shirt had food stains randomly applied by dirty fingers swiped across it like it was a napkin. His mouth felt cottony and he wondered what army just trampled through his mouth with dirty combat boots. *When was the last time I brushed my teeth?*

Tracey appeared in the mirror, leaning against the door frame. She didn't look any better. He turned and looked at her.

"What the...?" was all he could think of to ask. "How long have we been like this?"

Tracey stared as though in a trance, and Josh felt like giving her a 'Hollywood' slap, the one they used in movies to bring someone out of a daze. "What's happing to us" she managed to get out, almost choking on the words.

Josh resisted an overpowering urge to push her aside and get back to the story. The fedora was like a narcotic to him now. He had to have more. He saw Tracey turn and look back, realizing she was having similar feelings.

"Baby, we need to get out of here for awhile. We need to talk-"

He never finished, Tracey was suddenly sitting at the keyboard, talking to Remington and putting the fedora on. He watched her insert the next blank sheet of paper and was amazed at the frenzy of her typing. He put on his hoodie and ball cap, stood at the door for a moment and walked out of the apartment, leaving behind the rhythmic sound of her typing.

chapter

TWENTY NINE

Blaze gradually accustomed herself to the daily routine of the village. She was adding words to her growing vocabulary. She was still resorting to pantomime and pointing, but less and less as the days passed. One morning after a fierce wind and rain storm swept through in a rage, people emerged from their huts to find the central fire washed away.

"What will we do? Everything is too wet." They all sounded anxious. Everyone let their hut fires burn out during the night after the evening meal, not needing them for warmth. They all expected to rekindle their fires from the central fire pit.

Listening to the complaining about breakfast with cold food brought a smile to her face. She was a woman used to eating cold food as her people broke camp in the mornings, often without the benefit of using precious fire fuel for breakfast when they could simply chew on dried meat and berries for the sustenance they needed.

Blaze, however, came to learn how much these people depended on routine. Each day needed to be much like the day before, their patterns changing only with the seasons, not the days. Since the central fire always burned, it took no special skill to keep it going. Even the small children knew how to stoke it with wood and keep it burning.

"I will do it," she said. Her words were halting, still spoken with uncertainty in this new language. She waved people away from the central fire pit, handed her son to one of the women gathered around, and began using her fire starting skills.

It wasn't much of a challenge for her, knowing precisely what was needed. She pointed to the nearest hut and told the young boy what she needed. He came back with a pile of dried grass. Another boy brought small pieces of dried wood, used to feed the smaller hut fires, from another hut, and soon she made sure the central fire was started once again.

There were cries of *ooh* and *aah* as they watched the blaze grow until it was hot enough to accommodate a few pieces of the wet wood lying nearby drying in the heat. The rain passed too quickly to soak the wood all the way through and she knew it would burn easily once it caught.

While she was working, she heard her new son cry out, but the women gathered around to soothe his cries. A wet-nurse took the baby and began feeding him. Blaze was no longer amazed at the way these people worked as a group. The jobs within the clan here weren't as set in stone as with her desert people, but someone always seemed to know what was needed and did it.

The men each came by and patted her on the shoulders in appreciation as they picked up tools and walked to the nearby fields. The old woman, who Blaze now realized was the village elder, pulled her aside when the fire was fully engaged. They were both growing more comfortable in conversation, the words building between them.

"That was good," the woman said, and Blaze felt a glow of pride and appreciation at the praise, something seldom given in her former clan. "Where did you learn to do that?"

Blaze told her about her desert people. She explained, "I was the fire keeper," and told the woman about the importance of fire to their nomadic existence. She searched for the words to describe the job each member was assigned, how the responsibilities were passed from one generation to the next. She told about the hunter, the trackers and the beaters. She told about the women who turned animal skins into clothes, and all the jobs necessary for the desert people to survive.

"It sounds like a hard life."

Blaze never thought about that before. *Was it hard? I never thought of it that way, it was just the way it was.*

"I was given a name," Blaze said. I am Fire Starter. They call me Blaze."

"The woman laughed and taught her the word in her new language. She got up and walked to the door and announced to the village that her name was Blaze, and that she would oversee the fires from now on. One by one, the people started to clap their approval. The men in the distance looked to see what the clamor was all about, as a young boy raced out to tell them. Soon, they too, were yelling their welcome and gratitude, waving their arms and tools in the air.

"What is your name?" she asked the old woman.

"I am the oldest person in our village. When that happens, you become either Mother or Father, depending. When my man died, I became Mother."

Suddenly, they heard wild shouting from a young voice in the near distance. Blaze instinctively looked over at her son, asleep on the shoulder of the young wet-nurse who still held him. She followed Mother across the camp to see what the commotion was about.

A young man was racing towards the village on a horse. She had never seen an animal move so fast, muscles rippling as the horse came to a shuddering stop, a light film of white, foamy lather on his coat. The young man continued to call for attention, and the men came rushing in from the fields to gather around.

They all listened in alarm, including Blaze. "The highland people are coming. They are only three villages away." Blaze heard the murmuring this news caused, but didn't realize exactly what it meant. Her mind sensed the anxiety emanating from those around her.

"I saw huts burning, people screaming, fleeing into the woods, trying to escape. I saw them grab two young girls before they raced off back towards the hills."

The women exchanged glances and knew what that meant, but Blaze couldn't comprehend the significance.

Mother leaned over and whispered to Blaze, "I will explain later."

The men were having an animated discussion. Blaze realized, with a fright, they were organizing a defense of the village. As a nomadic clan member, warfare was never a part of the life of her tribe. Disputes, when they happened to arise, were settled between elders of the clans, diplomatically. There was little in life for the nomadic clans to fight about. No one owned land and the clans were necessarily small for quick, light travel.

In her desert life, the trackers and beaters would pick up traces of other peoples long before they were ever a threat. The tribes in the desert each knew to avoid the other, in order to avoid conflict. When there was a dispute that could not be settled by the elder meeting, one man would be chosen from each tribe. They would have a ceremonial battle with many threatening gestures, loud grunting and waving of sticks. When the mock battle was over, one would be declared the victor and the other tribe would pack and move out, thus settling any argument. Never in her life had she known one clan to steal members of another. The idea and the consequences were too unimaginable for her to grasp.

Unfortunately, she realized the permanence of the village would not allow these people to simply pack and move on, as was the way of the nomadic life. They must stand and defend the village, a concept completely alien to Blaze. It was her first lesson in defining what it meant to claim territory.

Later that night, by the light of their hut fire, Mother told her about the highland people. They also had villages, but lacked proper soil and fields for raising crops. At first, they would bring game from their highland homes to trade for grain and vegetable crops. It worked well until one of the highland villages was unsuccessful at hunting game during a scarce winter. The people faced hunger and the highland men decided to ride to the low country and simply take what they needed. As things like this do, it soon escalated. They discovered it was easier to raid for food than it was to hunt for food, especially when the low country people seemed to lack the skills necessary for defending themselves.

On one particular raid, a young highland man saw one of the low country girls running for safety. He was at the edge of manhood, when his blood surged at the sight of a young woman, and he raced after her on his horse.

When he caught up to her, he jumped down and clubbed her, knocking her unconscious. He draped her over his horse, jumped on and rode off with her body flopping. That was the beginning of the dark period. Word slowly came back that the captured women were used for pleasure and breeding, often forced to do the unpleasant work in the villages and treated as outcasts and slaves. The offspring of the unions produced children with features that didn't favor either village. They too were treated with contempt and held little hope for any escape from their plight.

The expected raid didn't develop. An uneasy feeling still draped over the village, however.

Mother looked down at the new baby and gasped. What if this happened to this lusty young male child and his mother? Although these two were new to the tribe, they all agreed to accept the strangers who were no longer strangers. "We need a naming ceremony," she said with finality.

Before Blaze could question this, she was told that by giving the boy a name, it meant he would forever be a part of the village and family. "But he has no skill yet," Blaze started to protest. In her old life, one had to earn a name, which could only happen later in life. Until then, all children were simply referred to as "child."

"That isn't important," the old woman retorted.

The next morning, she announced at the central fire that there would be a naming ceremony that night for their newest member. She looked around at the excitement. There hadn't been a new child in several seasons. Mother saw the willingness of the people to accept the boy as one of their own, confirming what they had all agreed to informally. It was a strange thing to treat a stranger that way, but they sensed this boy was special. His mother had already proved her worth, and there was no doubt the boy would also be unique and special.

Mother failed to notice how two men standing at the edge of the crowd looked at each other. The look they exchanged was not a look of acceptance.

"I have waited for so long and now this brat comes along and takes my place," one said.

"We need to get word to the highlanders," the other one muttered.

chapter

THIRTY

Tracey was exhausted. She sat back looking at the fedora, resisting its narcotic tug on her mind. Some instinct told her to get up and walk away.

How did it get to be like this? I need to get a grip. This is starting to feel like a creepy, alien mind-melt movie.

She made a decision. It was time for an intervention, a self-imposed intervention, she thought, laughing at the idea. She felt grimy to a degree she never before allowed. She imagined the dried sweat caked under her arm pits mixed with old clumps of deodorant; it wasn't a pleasant image.

She shuffled into the bathroom and reached for her toothbrush and began brushing. The gel of the paste tasted minty and pleasant. She brushed, timing to make sure she went a full two minutes. Then she recharged with paste and kept brushing until the gritty covering of her teeth was completely gone, scrubbing her tongue until she almost gagged, ridding it of coffee and Chinese food residue (along with some other foreign matter). She ran her tongue over the newly polished enamel with satisfaction. The tart taste of the mouthwash completed the ablution. She gargled and rinsed her mouth again.

She stripped and looked in the full length mirror to the side. Her hair was uncombed, there was a grey film of dirt covering her skin, and her eyes were thoroughly bloodshot. She opened the tiny medicine cabinet and grabbed the eye drops, tilted her head back and splashed the eye drops one by one, three drops in each eye. When her eyes cleared, she rubbed her hands over her skin and felt wretched. She pulled the shower curtain back and turned the tap on full hot and waited until the tub was steaming, filling the entire bathroom with a cleansing mist. She adjusted the temperature to a bearable hot and stepped in, picked up the soap and started washing away the grime of the past few days. She ignored the voice over her shoulder, the one telling her that Remington was waiting: "Come back and type," it said.

The voice she chose to listen to was the one telling her to enjoy the moment, to luxuriate in the feeling of clean. It was what she needed more than anything at the moment. She stepped out of the shower and started to towel down when she stopped and turned back to the tub. Plugging the drain, she decided to fill the tub with hot water. When it was nearly full, she gingerly stepped in, and with one swift move, settled down into the deliciously hot water. As she leaned back, she touched the enamel, which was almost painfully cold to the touch despite the heat of the water. She kept turning the water to a hotter setting and watched her skin turn to a reddish lobster color. *Now* this *is luxuriating!* Her lips curved upwards, smiling at the thought.

It wasn't the same as a hot tub or a spa, but it was close enough to count. Soon her eyes closed and she allowed her fingers to explore her own body, unembarrassed at the feeling of arousal as her fingertips passed over the erotic parts of her body. She had no intention of getting herself off; just fully enjoying the moments she had alone with neither Josh nor the fedora looking over her shoulder. In fact, she was almost asleep, hand still clutched between her legs, when she heard the front door open and Josh called her name. She couldn't bring herself to answer his call, lost and mesmerized in her private, steaming oasis.

He was still calling her name when he opened the door to the bathroom and felt the blast of steam hit him full on and saw Tracey, naked in the tub.

"I'm afraid," he said. "I had to walk, to clear my mind."

"I needed to clear my mind too," she murmured.

She whispered to him how good she felt, so clean and relaxed. Her dreamy voice and eyes transfixed him and he let himself get pulled into her dream. She watched as he took off his clothes and stepped into the tub, facing her and sliding his body down, legs splayed along the outside of her body. He leaned back and sighed. For a long moment he simply laid there, unmoving. Then he fumbled for the bar of soap, eyes still closed and a satisfied cat-ate-the-canary grin locked upon his face.

"Let me," she said dreamily.

She started rubbing his body with soap, gently rubbing the grime away from his cheeks and forehead with her hands and a wash cloth. She used small, gentle circles to massage open the pores and lift away the dirt and oil. As she moved lower to wash his chest and belly, she noticed with a smirk that his penis was growing erect, and her hand moved lower, washing the inner side of his legs.

"And, what do we have here?" she snickered.

With an awkwardness that was highly erotic, they managed to accomplish their coupling in that crowded tub, the water sloshing over the brim, both laughing the entire time. Laughing delayed the orgasms, which only made them laugh harder. By the time the deed was accomplished, there was only half a tub of water left and it was tepid to say the very least.

They dressed in clean clothes from the dresser, and without discussion, left the apartment holding hands.

"I know just the place for a drink," Tracey said and laughed as they started down the street. The streetlights were just starting to flicker on.

"Let's give Mr. Remington a rest for the night," Josh agreed and thought about the single-malt scotch he was going to order.

They were more than a bit under the influence when they walked from the bar to a nearby restaurant, but their feeling of revival was intact, and they thoroughly enjoyed the meal, knowing someone else would take care of the dirty dishes this time. They ignored Remington and the whisper of the fedora when they got back home. They went straight to the bedroom and reveled in love-making that didn't require acrobatic maneuvering in a bathtub. With a loud-quiet squeal, Tracey cried out as Josh arched his back and finished.

"I love you, Trace," he said. "I love you more than I have ever loved anyone before. Not only that, but I need you. I need you to keep me grounded with this strange story and that crazy fedora-"

She stopped him from talking. "And I love you, Josh. No more talking. Just hold me tight and shut up. Remy will be there in the morning. We need to-"

But Josh didn't hear her, he was already asleep, his jaw open and a loud snore erupted to cut her off. Tracey laughed and was soon asleep curled beside him, in spite of the raucous snoring.

Over breakfast in the morning Josh said, "I'm in trouble at school. I need to go in. Will you...?" The question wasn't necessary. She nodded before he even finished

The narcotic pull was already overwhelming her as she agreed to sit with Remington for the day.

chapter

THIRTY
ONE

Blaze didn't know what to expect. Mother told her that all she was required to do was bring the baby to the fire circle as the sun was leaving the sky. Mother laid out a wrap and told Blaze how to wear it. She laid a shawl next to the baby and gave instructions for dressing the boy.

"This color and pattern means it is a boy name," she said laughing, but the sound that came out was more a cackling noise like the chickens that roamed the village than anything else. That throaty, scratchy laugh might have sounded harsh to a stranger, but somehow it was soothing to Blaze's ears.

Blaze walked on tenterhooks as the day progressed, nervous and anxious to begin the ceremony. When the baby was asleep, she went out to make sure the fire was tended, adding wood as needed. She checked on the baby again, then went to the stream and cleaned her wraps and those of the baby. She washed away the baby's urine and feces, accepting their presence as a natural part of life.

She was developing a taste for the prepared grains and vegetables of the agrarian community, but she still appreciated the gift of game. One of the young men was good at capturing nearby rabbits, bringing them to her and watching in amazement as she neatly skinned the animals and prepared them for cooking.

One day, he quietly asked her, "What does it taste like?"

She laughed and held some of the meat over the flame until it was crisp and sizzling. Handing it to him on a stick, she motioned for him to eat. She was amused at his reluctance, watching him hold it to his nose to smell it first. Then he held it to his mouth and tentatively touched it with the tip of his tongue. Finally, he nibbled off a small piece and took it between his teeth.

"Well," she laughed, "are you going to eat it or just chew it?"

He swallowed and a smile spread over his face. He wiped a drop of juice from the corner of his mouth and took a second bite. Soon he was finished.

"What do you think?"

He told her he wasn't sure. It tasted different to him, but maybe he liked it. A few days later, he was a regular at her hut fire. Blaze looked around at three of his friends that also joined the circle, enjoying the taste of cooked meat. They were also starting to preen for her attention, recognizing her value as a potential mate.

But tonight was the night for the naming ceremony. The entire village waited outside around the fire. The older men and women, those in their middle years, and, of course, the children, who were running around until Mother shushed them. They squatted on their haunches then and waited.

Mother brought out a large container and took out items, holding them up and turning so all could see. Their sight elicited excited murmurs. Several started chanting, words that were unfamiliar to Blaze.

A man came up and took something out of the container and chanted as he tossed it into the fire. It caused the fire to flare wildly and soon sparks were spitting into the air, spiraling higher as if reaching for the stars.

A strange moaning sound seemed to come from the stars overhead. Blaze realized, with a start, that she was hearing a voice; it was the voice of Stargazer. A flood of guilt swept through her, realizing she had not thought of him in days.

A woman was seized with rapture and started to whirl around the fire, shouting in a tongue known only to her. Finally, she came to a stop and looked down at the baby in Blaze's arms.

"The One," she said with finality. "He is The One, and will go by the name of Star."

People gasped. They all knew the promise. They were told to wait for 'The One.' It had been passed down from elders long gone, those people of the past upon whose shoulders they all stood.

"Eeeeyaah," someone shouted and the celebration began in earnest. Mother looked at Blaze with a new reverence, eyes sparkling with sacred knowledge. "I knew it when I first saw you. I knew and didn't know. I am so happy for you." Blaze had no idea what had just happened, why everyone was looking at her in awe.

But two men stood at the back, looking at each other. They were very nervous. "We made a big mistake," one said.

"I fear the same," the other said. "But it's too late, the raid is set. The danger of the earlier raid had not disappeared, only postponed.

꩜

The two men indeed made a serious mistake. One was named Masterson, the son of the tilling master. He always considered himself to be in the running to become leader of the village one day. The other, his friend, supported the idea and hoped to benefit by the election with special favors. He was a lazy sort who often looked for ways to avoid work. As Masterson's assistant, he would be the one handing out work assignments instead of performing them. He wasn't very bright and was easily led into the web Masterson spun. Now he was unsure of this latest plot to secure power. "Have we made a mistake?"

Masterson waited a long time before replying. "I'm not sure, but I think so. What if this new baby is The One of the Elder's prophesies?"

In a fit of jealous rage, Masterson went to the highland raiders' village. As he rode in he held out his hands in a gesture intended to disarm any hostility.

He asked to meet with the leader and told the highlanders about the mysterious woman who had appeared from nowhere, pregnant and ready to give birth. When the new baby was born, there had been rumors throughout the village that he was a special boy, destined to greatness.

The highland leader stroked his chin in thoughtfulness. He had heard the whispers of a great man who would become a leader of leaders, a ruler over all the villages. "Tell me more about your village." He listened while Masterson drew diagrams in the dirt, outlining each hut and pointed out the one where Blaze and the new baby lived.

Masterson was ambitious and had been convinced of the promise of leadership and didn't see any harm in a raid on his own village, a raid designed solely to kidnap the strange woman and her boy child. Who was she to him? He saw the woman and the boy as mere impediments to his future. They were not a part of his village family.

Now, however, as he watched the naming ceremony, he was seized with guilt, unsure about the actions he had taken. The ceremony was sacred and the new baby was now acknowledged as The One. If it were true, he might have just doomed his own people. Masterson's impetuous selfishness had placed the new boy, now called Star, in high peril, along with the rest of his village.

"Eeyah," he yelled and strode into the light of the naming ceremony. He confessed to his family and the village, prostrating himself before them. As he finished telling them all that he had done, all that he planned, some whispered of fleeing. They all knew what Masterson refused to see: the highlanders would not stop at simply taking the girl and her son; they would devastate the entire village and make slaves of all those they caught.

"It is too late; the raid will be at first light."

Agitated murmuring grew amidst the crowd. What could they do? Some said flee, some pressed for making a stand, despite the hopelessness of it.

It was Blaze who stepped forward first. She knew the people in the village were afraid of the dark. To her desert nomad past, the dark was not to be feared, but used as an advantage. It took some convincing, but she gradually outlined a strategy that might work. She told the older boys and the oldest men to form a loose ring around the far perimeter of the village. They would shout and make noise to sound the alarm, but remain hidden from sight during the raid. She showed them all how to use the stars to navigate in the dark and helped assuage their fear of things that go bump in the night.

She set a second ring of defenders, closer to the village, made up of the rest of the men, the strongest—just in case. They would also cry out the alarm, passing the warning along, but would not engage in fighting unless they had to. They would stand just out of the firelight, still hidden in the field in the early dawn, warning of the raider's approach. She told both groups of alarm sounders how to fade and disappear from view after sounding the alarm.

Finally, she told all the rest to follow her. With some reluctance, the other villagers picked up a few necessary belongings and they all started to follow Blaze. She looked up at the stars and Stargazer for guidance. The people following her remained strangely silent, even the children. They walked until they reached the edge of the forest where the woods covered their retreat, swallowing them into an embrace of quiet safety.

Just as they stepped into the woods, Blaze looked up for Stargazer and saw a singular star, burning brightly, the light of a distant sun. She thought of her son's new name, Star. That would be *his* star, shining his destiny for the world to see.

Just before dawn, the distant alarm rang out and faded, carried on the gentle morning breeze. When the highlanders tore into the collection of huts on their large horses, built more for work than for raiding, they looked around the abandoned village. In their rage, they gathered up what they could carry off and set fire to the huts.

By the time the sun reached its zenith, the raiders were gone. The men who sounded the alarm slowly wandered back into the village among the ruined huts, openly crying at the loss. None had seen what became of the women and children and some were convinced they had all been carried off.

Then, from the direction of the woods, they saw a line of women and children snaking back towards the village with Blaze in the lead. The men counted, all the women and children were safe. When the women got to the village, they too joined in mourning, until Mother said quietly but firmly, "We rebuild, here."

In three days, the first of the huts were reconstructed and the most vulnerable—the children and the elderly—had a place to sleep. Temporary lean-tos provided shelter from the wind and a small comfort for the rest.

On the third night, they gathered in another ceremony, this time to give thanks to the mother of Star. She saved them from great grief. Blaze didn't know how to react. In her world, one simply did one's job, without thanks and without praise. She blushed as she accepted their gratitude and held up her new son, Star, for everyone to see. Someone started to chant and soon all that were able started to chant and dance in thanks and praise.

chapter

THIRTY
TWO

The apartment reverted to a state of high disorder and bordered on outright chaos. Tracey and Josh took turns sitting in front of Remington. The narcotic pull of the fedora was too great. When one was typing, the other was sleeping, exhausted. They were being consumed by a story that neither truly understood. At one point, Tracey even gave voice to her doubts that it was even true, but Josh dissented, convinced it was a distant echo of a forgotten past.

They both agreed the whole thing was totally weird. But they couldn't get away from it. In the back of his mind, Josh even started to wonder what would happen when the story was finished. If the fedora had another story in it, he wasn't sure they would survive it.

Josh woke up one morning and reached for his cell. He flipped it open only to see the warning the battery was dead. He plugged in the charger and it wasn't long before the phone started chirping. Voice and text messages accumulated while the battery was dead. Josh scrolled through and deleted all but one. He ignored and deleted the ones he didn't care to respond to, especially the pathetic messages from Kelsey. He was shocked at feeling a murderous rage towards her and her creepy, "I need you," texting.

One voice mail message he didn't delete was from his faculty advisor, advising he *had* to call. Josh looked at the calendar and realized, to his horror, that he missed a whole lot of classes—most of the semester, in fact.

With dread, he pressed call and waited for his advisor to answer. Josh listened, turning a shade of pale, and finally flipped the phone shut without so much as a good-bye.

"I've been thrown out of the program, out of school." He threw the phone against the kitchen wall and watched the pieces of electronic components and plastic scatter. Again!

Tracey barely looked up. She was getting ready to put on the fedora and her face had the look of an addict, stretched thin, preparing for a new injection of heroin.

She put on the hat and started typing, hunched forward in her chair.

Josh curled up on the tile floor, knees drawn up, and he was sobbing. *What is going on?*

Tracey finished the next page and pulled out the paper, turning it upside down on the growing manuscript pile. She inserted a clean sheet and started typing again, never breaking focus.

chapter

THIRTY
THREE

The seasons turned one by one until Star had grown into an older boy, almost a man. The village went through many changes, yet remained mostly the way it always been. There were times of plenty when they would celebrate with thanksgiving. There were times of scarcity when the people preserved precious resources, using them sparingly. The weather cycled through calm and storm, never upsetting the overall balance nature maintained.

Then Mother Elder died and great keening followed her death. She was loved by most and respected by all. No one ever challenged her place at the head of the village.

The two men who had given the highlanders the idea of the long-past raid rode off one day, never to be seen again. Masterson couldn't stand by watching the reverence given to Star, nor the ever-growing looks of chastisement thrown his way.

To his credit, Star never asked for, nor received, any special treatment. He was a hard and tireless worker in the fields, often helping the older workers who had trouble keeping up. He displayed a disarming personality, and few could resist his lopsided grin.

His mother also passed along her special skills to him, the skills she learned as a nomad on the far side of the mountain. However, some instinct preserved inside her led her to teach these skills in secret. As one who possessed secret knowledge, he came to be accepted as a person with great powers. Then, as was true in all the days of recorded history to follow, knowledge was the key to power, to be used for good or for ill, depending on the one who possessed it.

Star grew restless as he approached the day of his manhood initiation ceremony. He was careful not to wake his mother, slipping through the opening of the hut and walking into the high grasses, disappearing during the predawn hours. Blaze wasn't asleep and knew of his leaving, knowing also that he needed to be alone and did not need an admonition to be careful.

The boy would find a level spot and lie down, looking up at the fading stars in the heavens, as if waiting for instructions. He knew the location of Stargazer in the western sky and wondered at his own star blinking brightly near to Stargazer's constellation. He looked up in acceptance of the knowledge that flowed to him from the stars.

The village seemed to have ceremonies for all occasions. The naming ceremony set someone on a path at birth; thanks for the harvest ceremony showed gratitude for the bounty of food provided by Mother Nature. The farewell ceremony, especially for Mother's passing, was a moving reminder that life, all life, had an end to the cycle of seasons.

The ceremony initiating young men and women into the fullness of village membership was eagerly anticipated by all the boys and girls. They emerged from that ceremony as men and women, like butterflies thrusting out and breaking free from their chrysalis, shedding the cocoon of childhood. These newly appointed adults were eager to spread their wings and show their worth.

The chanting and dancing drew to an end of the ceremony for Star. The frenzy of celebration gave way to an excited weariness, and slowly the villagers took their seats around the fire. They awaited the speech the newly acknowledge member was expected to deliver. Most, if not all, stayed true to form: "I pledge myself to the village and promise to work hard," etc. The villagers grew quiet in anticipation of hearing the words from Star.

"It is time for me to leave," they heard the words in disbelief. A gasp went up and there were shouts of "no, no," from many in the circle. Some women started to weep openly, especially the young ones who dreamed of becoming his wife one day, and who competed for his attention. But Star raised his hand to quiet the villagers.

"My mother carried a seed from a distant land, a seed that grew to maturity in this village. You accepted her without question. For that, I will be forever grateful." He paused, and the sounds of quiet sobbing continued around the central fire.

"I had a vision," he said, looking at his mother. She nodded with understanding, one of the few whose cheeks were free of tears. She suspected this might happen. She watched his restlessness. She, like none of the others, knew there was a much larger world beyond the low country villages and the places where the highlanders lived. Her son was a part of this new place, but she also knew he was a child of the nomadic blood and would never escape his preordained destiny.

"Where will you go? What will you do?" The questions flew around the circle of people, still disbelieving what they were hearing.

"I wish I could answer your questions," Star said. "There are things beyond our understanding. The stars have told me to seek out that which we do not know. There are many ways of doing things. I need to find out why the highlanders choose one way, while we chose another. Sometimes, we all get to the same place by following different paths. Why is that and what does it mean for us? I do not have the answers."

Blossom, a young daughter of one of the field workers, had not yet qualified for her turn at the coming-of-age ceremony. She just experienced the first bleeding cycle and the older women had taken her to a hut to explain the cycle of blood and birthing. Though they knew details, none fully understood all of the connections. But they helped ease her pain with soothing balms and massage.

She wasn't supposed to speak, her status still that of a child, but she couldn't hold back. She believed she was destined to be the wife of this extraordinary man, Star. She stood and walked up to Star.

"Take me with you." It wasn't a question.

Star looked at her for a long time, considering what she demanded of him. Finally, he agreed. "Yes. I feel this is to be."

The villagers gasped; Blossom hadn't taken part in her ceremony yet. It wasn't possible for her to be with a man. Yet, something about the scene before them told them all traditions would see upheaval before this young man was through. They hushed once more.

"I love you all," he said, spreading his hand out and waving it broadly. "I am leaving on this journey for the good of the tribe, and Blossom will leave with me. We will be away for a long time, many planting and harvesting seasons."

"No," women cried. Some men cried as well.

"Don't cry for me," he admonished. "Do not cry. This is something that must be done and it is something to be embraced with hope and joy, not sorrow. For when I return, I will bring answers. I will return with my destiny."

He turned to his mother and knelt in front of her. He put his hand gently under her chin and tilted her head up. He saw tears finally streaming from her eyes.

"My dear mother, you have travelled far and seen much. You have been given gifts even you do not understand. They were all for a purpose. Stargazer told me that you will have a full life, but you will no longer be among the living when I return. Always know that your gifts and love will sustain me always." He couldn't bear seeing the pain mixed with joy in her eyes, and turned to address Blossom's own mother.

"Know, as well, Mother of Blossom, that your daughter is destined for greatness. Celebrate that in your remaining days. You have given her a special gift of vision that allowed her to see her calling and stand up to that challenge, even before the ceremony of adulthood."

The last memory Star and Blossom had of the village was the sight of their two mothers embracing in the fire's light. The following morning, before the rooster's crowing, Star and Blossom walked out of the village and did not look back. Their resolute steps carried them toward their future.

chapter

THIRTY FOUR

Tracey was unable to stop crying as she finished this part of the story. The words ricocheted around in her head and she thought about the story long after she took the fedora off.

She rushed into the living room, shaking Josh awake. He was sprawled on the sofa, one leg over the back, the other draped down, his foot on the floor.

"It's beautiful and sad at the same time," she explained, telling Josh about Star and Blossom.

"Who the hell is Blossom?"

She watched him rub sleep away and ignored his question. "He is leaving and Blossom is going with him."

"Where?"

"I don't know, but I have to find out. I need to rest, first. Start typing. It's your turn with Remington," she said, pulling him off the sofa, urging him into the kitchen with gentle pushes from behind.

"I'm hungry," he complained.

Tracey ran to the refrigerator and started making sandwiches. She put two on a paper plate and placed a glass of milk alongside, ignoring the faint odor that indicated the contents was on the verge of spoiling.

She brushed her hair as best she could and just reached the door, on her way to get groceries, when Josh exclaimed, "Oh no," the dismay in his voice was alarming.

She returned to the kitchen and saw him frantically trying to lift the cover and find out what was jamming the carriage. "It won't budge. I can't type," and he started to pound on Remington.

"Get your laptop," he said to Tracey. She carried it from the other room and set it down next to Remington. Josh put on the fedora and his fingers were soon poised over the laptop keyboard. "Nothing," he said, looking up at her in wide-eyed terror, "not a word."

He turned back to Remington and touched the key pads, frantically trying to make them work. Remington wouldn't budge, however. "I hear the words though," he said. "But they are stuck, like a record on a turntable that just keeps stuttering the same word without moving on.

"Who knows how to fix something like this typewriter? Is there anyone who still knows how to make repairs on something like this? Hand me the phone book," he said.

After fanning through the phone book he called several shops that claimed to repair typewriters, but they all added that their expertise was limited to later models, all electric typewriters.

Josh and Tracey were like two drug addicts long past the need for a fix. Desperation flashed between them like a neon sign. Josh began to stutter, barely able to speak. Tracey lost her composure completely and started crying uncontrollably. Josh never saw that part of her until now, and he wasn't impressed. She looked at the wildness in his eyes and was likewise unimpressed with what she was seeing.

"There is one last number," he said hopelessly, and reached for the phone. There was long wait until someone finally answered. Josh listened and nodded. Then he listened some more and described the problem when prompted. "Wait a sec," he said and handed the phone to Tracey to hold.

He turned Remington over and there it was—a paperclip was jammed in the platen, stopping the carriage from working back and forth. He took the phone back from Tracey and described what he found. "I'll try," He said into the phone.

He rooted in drawers until he found long-nosed pliers. He carefully pulled on the paperclip and finally loosened it enough to pull it completely out. He tested Remy, who once again worked with its old mechanical reliability.

"How much do I owe you," he said into the phone, surprised and pleased when he heard, "nothing," as the reply.

"Advice is free," he told Tracey, his laughter almost hysterical.

There came a knock on the door. "Is anyone home," a voice yelled, the knocking continuing.

"Who is-?" Josh started to say.

"It sounds like Suzanne," Tracey said moving toward the entryway.

She opened the door and the two women screamed and started hugging each other like nine-year-olds.

"I've been trying to find you forever!" Suzanne said.

"How *did* you find me?"

"Phillip at the bar said to look here."

Suzanne looked around the apartment in disbelief. "My god, what a mess. No, wait…that doesn't begin to describe this, it's beyond mess."

Suzanne turned to Tracey, "And you look awful, girl. You look absolutely dreadful." Suzanne turned to examine Josh, and was far from impressed. *All the men at her feet and this she ends up with?* She kept that thought to herself, however.

Josh realized that Tracey was steering her friend away from the story. She was keeping Suzanne from the kitchen. She told Josh later she knew it would be dangerous for anyone else to know what was happening.

Suzanne looked hurt when Tracey suggested she leave, even with the promise of a girl's night out in the near future. "I don't even have a number to call," she complained, as Tracey walked her to the stairs.

"I'll call you," Tracey promised.

Tracey closed the door and turned to Josh. "We can't let anyone else see this. We have to keep this whole mess a secret."

Josh nodded his understanding and then had a thought. He knew of a vacant loft for rent in an area not far away. It was in a warren of artist studios, and artisans were all thought to be eccentric anyway. "I may have an idea."

After they rented the studio, they moved Remy, the fedora, the manuscript and all their necessary supplies to what they called the "writing room."

"This is where we will write from now on," Josh said and Tracey agreed. There was a sink in a skanky bathroom at the end of the hall. "At least we can make coffee," she said as Josh plugged in the coffee maker and hot plate.

The next day, he browsed a used furniture stores until he located a daybed. The two of them managed to lug it back to the studio balanced on a shopping cart, looking like refugees in a World War Two newsreel.

They looked around their new writing sanctuary and were pleased with the results. Tracey locked the door and they returned to the apartment. Once again they rehabilitated the flat, salvaging some semblance of order from the chaos they created. They both showered and worked at looking presentable, a major achievement.

"That was close with Suzanne," Tracey said.

"Yah, we can't let anyone know what is happening with this whole story thing," Josh agreed.

They ordered in Chinese, and for the first time in a long time, settled in with one of the movies from Josh's collection of old DVDs.

The next morning, Josh said he was going to try and talk to someone at school. "It may be impossible," he said, "but I have to try to get back in." He watched Tracey sipping coffee and thought, once more, how lucky he was to have her in his life, despite what the last few weeks had done to them both. "I made some sandwiches. They're in the cooler. I put in a soda and an apple, too."

"You're so thoughtful," she said with an honest smile.

Josh was putting on his hoodie when he turned around and said, "I will meet you at the studio when I'm done." He walked his bicycle out the door and was soon pedaling his way to the university campus.

Tracey had a spring in her step as she walked to the studio, carrying the cooler and listening to her playlist on her MP3 player.

The old building felt strange to her. Most of the artisans seemed to work odd hours and weekends. It was quiet, almost eerie, for a weekday morning. The ancient hallway floor creaked underfoot and she thought she could hear the old walls breathing. The lighting was poor on the top floor, and the freight elevator groaned in protest as it rose slowly. The only light came from two bare bulbs at each end of the hallway, hanging from twisted wires dangling from the ceiling.

Tracey tried to ignore the shadows, shadows that seemed to move as she turned to look around. *My imagination is working overtime.* She wasn't entirely convinced it was her imagination that caused the shadows to move, however.

Once in the room, she turned on the overhead light and walked over to the window. It hadn't been opened in ages, and it took some persuading to finally dislodge the bottom pane. When she slid it up to the top, she realized it wouldn't stay there on its own. She located one of Josh's books and placed it under the window, propping it open. The room seemed to breathe in the fresh air, as if it were an old friend that hadn't visited in a long time.

She turned on a side lamp they brought to furnish the room, placing it next to Remington. She smiled and touched the case of the typewriter lovingly. She completed the ritual of preparation, paper in place and ready, and sat down.

"Well," she said aloud. "Let's have a go, shall we?"

Soon the fedora sat askew on top of her head and her fingers were leaping from key to key, the rhythm of her typing back to a familiar speed.

chapter

THIRTY
FIVE

Star kept looking up at the night sky and adjusting their course as needed. Blossom had the old villager fears of the dark and the unknown and hurried to keep pace with Star whenever she lagged behind. She watched Star look up from time to time and mutter under his breath. She sensed it was not a time for questions and accepted his leadership. She guessed, rightly, her learning would be a gradual thing and he would be her teacher when the time came.

Blossom was entering her woman's stage of life. It was a time of wonder for her, and yet she admitted to her inner voice that she was frightened and often dreamt about what might be in store for her during the coming years. Some of those dreams were nightmares, but she pushed them aside when they happened. Her emotional range was widening. She had a feeling of warmth towards the man walking ahead, his shoulders broad, his hair long and his legs strong.

She first interpreted her feelings towards him as love, and wondered what it would be like when they consummated their union. Her mother told her about that before she left, a secret normally kept until the night of the union ceremony. But the farther from the village they walked, the clearer her emotions seemed to her. This man would not be the father of her children. He would never be her mate. He was needed by all men and women. She couldn't hold him to her in a greedy clutch. Then what was she feeling? What was her attraction to this man? She shook her head absently. She only knew that there was something reverential about him. It was a sensation that drew her to him like a moth to a flame.

But unlike the unwary moth that dove headlong into the flame, Blossom would not end up consumed and destroyed by it, but would take energy from the fire she could see burning inside of Star. She would follow him, be his companion, and accept what life gave her.

"It's funny," he said, "The first time I saw you, I had a feeling we shared a destiny." He stopped and looked back at her. "There will be others who will join us. We are going to be a new kind of family, a people neither desert nor village."

Blossom didn't know what to say, and so said nothing. She waited. Patience was a virtue that she relied on.

Star proved to be adept at finding game. He learned the skill from his mother. Blossom was a villager and was more accustomed to the grainy food of the low country, but the taste of game was growing on her, pungent and wild. She complimented their food supply with her ability to process the grains as they travelled. Often, when game was scarce, she would open her pouch and produce some bread product, perfect for dipping in the hearty soups she scrounged together out of wild herbs and root vegetables.

There was a point when she looked back from a higher elevation, feeling timid. She never travelled this far from her home, and when she looked back over the lower country, she couldn't make out any of the details. The familiar terrain around her village gave way to the foothills they were in. She looked to the south, to the high mountains. She could make out the ragged outline and the clouds depositing large amounts of snow on their peaks.

"No need to worry," Star told her one day. "The mountains we are heading towards are the low mountains. They are covered with trees, nearly to the top. You can see them," he said, and pointed away to the right, "green, the color of life. Game and grain is in ample supply there."

She looked in the direction he was pointing and agreed the mountains weren't as steep, more like gentle foothills sloping up to rounded tops. She spotted three deer in a clearing ahead, a large stag with great antler racks accompanied by two does.

"Animals like that offer good skin for clothes and our shelters," she said.

"We will take what we need to survive and leave the rest," he said, echoing his mother's philosophy.

"Are there dangerous animals? I have heard of such things," she said, "animals with sharp teeth and claws that can rip a man or woman in half."

"There are dangers. We will give wide berth to those creatures. They are only looking for the food they need, as do we. But there is no need to fear."

When they made camp each night, Star would make the fire, "In honor of my mother, the Fire Starter," he would always say. He made the fire quickly—a small fire for the warmer nights and a larger one for those nights when the rainy mist would seep into the campsite on cat's paws.

As they walked higher into the smaller mountains, it grew cooler. It wasn't cold enough for snow, but Blossom knew the season of the short days and long nights was approaching. The nights were growing colder and Blossom would often move her sleeping skin closer to the fire.

She took comfort from the sight of Star sitting guard. He sometimes appeared to be asleep, nodding to the night air. She knew from experience, however, that he was alert to any sounds out of place in the night. She once watched him snap fully awake, and then smile as an animal that looked like a dog wandered into the light of the fire.

"A wolf," Star told her. "There are others nearby. This one is here to observe and report back. We will not threaten this animal." The wolf sat back on haunches and cocked its head in curiosity. Finally, as if bored with the sight, the wolf got up, walked in a tight circle and trotted into the night with one final glance over its shoulder.

"How do you know such things?"

"My mother told me about a wolf that walked with her once, before I was born." He didn't tell her he often sensed knowledge flowing from the stars. He didn't tell her about Stargazer and his part in the journey.

They had been walking for several days when they encountered two men. Star saw them and continued walking in their direction. He held up his hands to them to indicate he was unarmed and not a threat.

The two stood on the edge of a clearing and watched Star and Blossom draw closer. One raised a large stick in his hand and motioned for the travelers to stop. He spoke in a dialect that was unrecognizable to Blossom. She shook her head in amazement when Star spoke in the same language. Blossom picked up some words, but more importantly, she watched the two men visibly relax.

"They are hunters," Star told her.

"The one on the right is the leader, the brave. The other one is learning. He is younger."

Blossom looked at the two strangers and waited.

"Show them some food," Star told her.

Soon, the four were squatting around a small fire burning in the center of their little camp, the two men tearing pieces of meat, showing their gratitude with wide grins.

"How far have you come in your hunt," Star asked them.

"Our village is three days," pointing to the north and east. "We are looking for game to store for the snowy season."

"What are you doing here," the younger one finally asked. Perhaps he was the braver of the two after all.

"We are looking for a passage to the future."

The two young hunters looked at each other and then closely at Star. "Where will you find such a passage?" the younger one asked. "We have travelled far and wide and all we see are the green trees," waving his hand in a sweeping gesture.

"The passage I seek is not a mark you can make in the dirt with a stick."

The older one surprised them all by turning to Star. "I want to go with you. I want to find such a passage." The way he said it left little doubt that such a passage existed. He was drawn to join the expedition.

He turned to the younger man and gave him explicit instructions. He was to return to their village with the game they stored in a nearby tree. He was to carry it back to the village with the news that he was now called "Searcher," and he would not be coming back.

The young hunter didn't understand, but he nodded his acceptance and the next morning, trotted off to the east with the meat they cached in the hollow tree. The three who remained cleaned away their presence from the campsite, and when the sun was well above the horizon started to walk.

During the night Star watched the heavens for a sign. He led them north and to the west. He guided them to a low point between two rounded mountain tops. It was a pass where the trees gave way to a grassy meadow, alive with birds and butterflies busy taking advantage of the waning autumn sun.

chapter

THIRTY SIX

Tracey sat back, the fedora resting on top of the manuscript pile, thinking, *what an odd turn to the story.*

She never bothered with a wrist watch. Time didn't mean much to her these days. No school, no job—nothing of importance but the story living inside her head. The cell chirped and when she flipped the lid she was surprised to see how late it was.

"Talk to me," she said. She knew it was Josh calling.

"It's going better than I expected. I may be back in class after all."

She knew it was important, somehow, but really couldn't muster much enthusiasm. "Yah," was all she said.

"How's..." a pause, "the story going?"

She hesitated, and Josh didn't press her for any details.

"Should I come to the studio or meet you at the apartment," he asked.

"Here," she said. "I'm at the studio. I want you to read this latest part and tell me what you think. Then I think we should leave it for the night."

Josh caught the weary tone in her voice.

"See you, baby. I'll bring pizza."

Tracey closed the phone. She was having a hard time concentrating her thoughts and didn't pick up the fedora, even though the urge to do so was there. She put on her ear buds and scrolled through to her favorite playlist. Soon the soundtrack to *Eccentricities of a Blond Hair Girl* was curling inside her head. The music segued to *Three Trapped Tigers*, a UK trio she heard about from a girl friend. It was oddly soothing to her. Josh listened to it and screwed up his face, saying he didn't get it.

Tracey nodded to the music and looking at the window, realized it was already late afternoon, much later than she realized, Josh's phone call seemed a distant memory. That explained the hunger pangs, and she wondered how much longer before Josh arrived with the pizza. *Should I call and remind him to pick up a bottle of wine?* She suspected he would remember and so didn't bother to pick up the cell.

As if on cue, it started to chirp again. She flipped it and scrolled to the waiting text, "On the way pizza & wine."

Tracey stretched and leaned back in the chair. Suddenly restless, she stood up and walked down the hall to the bathroom. It was filthy, uncomfortable-looking stains where they shouldn't be, and no toilet paper. She cursed under her breath, forgetting to bring something to wipe with. She needed to piss too badly and had to overcome her revulsion. She couldn't bring herself to touch her ass to the toilet seat, and so squatted down, hovering above it until she was finished. Her jeans would just have to soak up the remaining drops.

She pushed down on the handle and the toilet didn't flush. "Shit," she said. There was no one to hear her. She looked at the tank, grimacing with the task ahead. Screwing up her courage, she lifted the tank lid and reached into the disgusting looking pool of water, finding and tripping the flushing mechanism. The water swirled and she watched it circling the bowl and plunging into the depths of the unseen but definitely appreciated sewer system. At least, she hoped that was where it went. She pushed the brief glimpse of dead bunnies and squirrels along some remote waterway out of her head.

She was walking back down the hallway to the studio when she heard the ancient freight elevator groaning its way to her floor. The gate lifted and Josh stepped out. He was balancing a pizza box in one hand, a bottle of wine in the other. "I even remembered to get a corkscrew," he said with a grin, gesturing with his chin toward his pocket.

They hugged once Tracey took the bottle off his hands. "Damn," she said. "Did you also remember to get some glasses?" She saw his face and was sorry she said anything. She thought that fleeting look of inadequacy that passed over his face was a lingering legacy of Kelsey's constant harping. *Bitch probably scarred him for life...*

They sat cross-legged on the floor eating slices of pizza from the open box. They passed the wine bottle back and forth, washing down the meal. Josh had the manuscript by his side and was leaving grease stained fingerprints as he carefully tried to turn the pages. "Incredible!"

As if by mutual agreement, once Josh finished, they steered their conversation away from the story, letting it marinade.

"What happened at school?"

"I'm on probation, can you believe it?"

"What does that mean?"

"I can't miss any more classes and I have to do papers on mathematics and the economy."

Tracey was incurious; she only asked to be polite. "I'm not sure I can go on," she said finally, meaning the story.

She felt better for saying it. She was feeling the narcotic pull of the fedora once again and wanted to embrace it, but remained determined not to.

"We have to leave," she said resolutely, scooping up the pizza box, corkscrew and bottle and started toward the door. Josh raced to keep up with her.

At the apartment, their approach to making love was anything but a success. Finally, they both agreed it was sleep they needed. They turned their backs to each other, each lost in thought and concern. Finally, Josh turned, and spooning Tracey, he draped his arm over her soft body. "Should we stop the writing?"

"Shhh," Tracey replied. She turned and put her fingers against his lips. "It will be better in the morning."

And it was. Josh told her he had to be on campus and asked her if she was going to the studio. She nodded, chewing a peanut butter sandwich, gulping milk. "Despite everything I said last night, everything this damned hat has done to us, I have to know. Besides, the NANOWRIMO month is just about up, so we might as well try and finish. I'd hate to be this close and just throw it all away. I've never been a quitter and I don't intent to start now."

Josh tried to hug her as he left and she held back, something she had never done before. He was troubled by her resistance as he biked to school. Tracey was also troubled by her own reaction as she walked to the studio and up the stairs to open the door. Remington and the mysterious hat were waiting for her. And so were Star and Blossom.

chapter

THIRTY SEVEN

Star led the way. Searcher and Blossom followed without question. Searcher told her one night that he recognized Star from a dream. Their village also heard about The One. Blossom nodded and told him the story she had been told as a child, about the arrival of a stranger, a woman ready to give birth. People said she would have an aura that would disappear once 'The One' was born. Some claimed they saw it on Blaze and now surrounding Star when the light was just right.

Star sat off to the side, listening to their conversation and smiling. As expected, when Searcher joined them on this journey, the young man would now preen and try to attract the attention of the fair Blossom. She lived up to her name; she was a truly blossoming flower as she approached womanhood. Star watched her slowly giving in to the man's attention. Nature would take its course with these two.

His thoughts were interrupted by a sound, a small twig snapping. Neither Blossom nor Searcher heard it above their conversation, but Star was attuned to the slightest warning sounds. He stood up and stepped back unnoticed into the shadows, beyond the light of the fire.

Three men hurdled over a log and into the light, one seizing Searcher and the other leering at Blossom, who was too terrified to even scream. The third man lifted a heavy club and prepared for a blow to Searcher's head. Just as he lifted the club, a banshee scream pierced the night and Star suddenly appeared, swift and mysterious.

His hand chopped at the back of the club holder's neck and the man dropped to his knees, instantly dead. All turned at the sight, never having seen such a powerful blow. Star twisted his body, his foot flew to the side and the head of the second man crunched beneath the blow, the bone breaking with a sickening sound. Suddenly freed, Searcher was still paralyzed by what he saw.

The third man, holding Blossom, let go of her and started to run. His face registered pure panic. Star transferred a long piece of wood from his left hand to his right and with a graceful throw, the wood found its mark, piercing the fleeing thug in the back. The man turned slightly, the spear having penetrated completely. He stood for just a moment with a look of surprise and then sank to his knees and seized the spear sticking through his chest with both hands, wracking spasms gave way to a final gasp, and he, too, was dead.

When quiet returned, Searcher was rubbing his arm where he had been held. Blossom was on the verge of crying, yet fascinated with the lethal moves she had just seen Star employ. She shuddered at the thought of what might have been; it was a close thing. She had never seen a man kill another man.

Star stood in total calmness and said quietly, "We need to bury the bodies. They don't deserve to be food for scavengers."

Searcher looked disgruntled. "What honor do they have to deserve a burial? They would have killed me and taken the girl and-"

They all heard it at the same time. It was a whimper, coming from the darkness. Star picked up a log and placing it into the flames, ignited it to use as a torch. Blossom and Searcher followed with trepidation. Only Star seemed unfaltering.

A few meters into the darkness, they saw her cowering. Her hands and feet were bound with leather tethers. Her hair was snarled and dirty, and her face covered with mud. Her wrap was pulled up around her waist and her legs were drawn up to cover her immodesty. Without thinking, Blossom took off the skin she was wearing and covered the girl. She directed Searcher to find water. When he returned, Blossom began soothing the frightened creature, using the wet cloth to scrub away the caked mud. Blossom hummed a quiet song her mother used to sing to her as a child and felt the frightened creature start to relax.

Blossom was startled as she washed the inside of the girl's legs, encrusted with blood and dried semen. The three men lying dead had forced themselves on her. Blossom's anger rose into her throat, but she kept it down for the sake of the frightened girl. Star noticed the glazed look in the young woman's eyes, animal-like, willing away any memory of her past few days. He knew it was the way of some peoples—he heard the stories of the highlanders from his mother.

Star and Searcher formed a cradle with their entwined arms and carefully carried the girl back to the camp and the light of the fire. She shrieked an eerie scream when she saw the bodies of her captors, holding her hand to her mouth. She looked around, unable to quell her terror, fearing she might be next.

Blossom tried to talk to her in the village language, the low-country dialect. Every now and then, the girl seemed to recognize a word and finally started to speak. Blossom heard the words "mother," "sister" and a few other familiar words, but they were disjointed and they formed no coherent story in Blossom's mind. Blossom could only shake her head in confusion. The girl began to cry wracking sobs and drew her knees up to her chest with her hands over her face. Blossom did the only thing she knew to do: she dropped alongside the girl and took her in her arms, muttering soothing words and humming a melody.

It was the melody that worked. The girl quieted and looked at Blossom, cocking her head to the words. She reached up with her hand, her fingers to Blossom's cheek. Then she turned and clasped onto Blossom, gave a heaving sigh and closed her eyes, a comforting sleep embracing her. Exhaustion outweighed her fear.

By the time the sun peeked over the horizon, Star and Searcher cleaned away all signs of the previous day's struggle and removed the intruders' bodies. They buried them despite Searcher's disapproval.

The three travelers squatted on their heels and patiently waited for the young girl to awaken. She awoke abruptly, giving a short scream and sat up. She drew her arms in front of her in a defensive posture, as though waiting for a blow to strike her. Her eyes darted around the scene and finally came to rest on Star. He stood, passive, knowing she was still in shock. He nodded to Searcher, who handed bread and water to Blossom.

She put her arm around the young girl and soothed her while offering nourishment. The girl looked at the food. She lifted it to her nose tentatively, sniffing, then tasted the bread with the tip of her tongue and was soon devouring everything she was given.

"She hasn't been fed in days," Star said, watching.

"I wonder if she has a name," Searcher said.

Blossom was adamant. "Her name will be Fortuity." Neither man was prepared to disagree. They looked at each other and nodded their approval. It was chance that brought them together, and it was chance that saved her from a life as a slave.

Their little group had now grown to four.

That night, preparing for the next leg of their journey, Star remained apart and meditated. He slowed his thinking and breathing to allow the voices from the past to catch up to him. He heard the voices of Stargazer and his mother. They urged him on, to follow the road to his true destiny.

chapter

THIRTY EIGHT

Tracey finished typing, barely able to see the keyboard. Day turned into night, and she had not eaten since breakfast. Her stomach let out a growl of protest, demanding food. She looked at the half-empty cup on the table and realized she was drinking too many cups of caffeine. She was wired, tired and ravenously hungry.

She looked around the studio and there was nothing to eat, not even a candy bar or bag of chips.

Where is Josh? Her irritation bubbled to the surface, like crude oil in a tar pit. But, before she could summon another nasty thought about Josh, she heard him stumbling in the hallway.

"What happened to the lights? I can't see a flippin' thing," Josh shouted. She heard him stumble into the wall and curse, "Damn it to hell. I had to walk up the stairs."

Tracey couldn't help it. She giggled hearing Josh smack face-first into the plaster wall. What wasn't so funny, however, was that she was suddenly aware of how dark it was getting, and there were no lights on in the studio. "The power must be off," she mumbled to herself.

"No shit," his words dripping with sarcasm. Josh stood there in the entryway, having opened the door unnoticed while Tracey was giggling, wrapped up in the picture of Josh stumbling down the hallway. She had the good sense to stand up and make her way toward his shadowy figure next to the door. They hugged and Josh finally said, "Well, this is just dandy."

With no ambient light from the street-side windows and no lights in the studio, it was growing pitch dark. They stood and tried to decide what to do.

Remington and the hat would have to wait. They felt their way out to the hall, rubbing their hands along the wall until they were at the stairway.

"Hey," Tracey said and started feeling her way back. "I forgot to lock."

They finally made it to the street, and except for car lights, it was obvious the power outage affected more than just their scruffy little writer's studio. They walked to a pizzeria, intending to grab a bite before they realized it, too, was without power. The servers and cooks were standing at the front door, at a loss for what to do.

There is something undeniably romantic about a blackout. There is also something a little frightening. Josh and Tracey walked towards their apartment, passing a convenience store along the way. The owner, at his enterprising best, was standing in the doorway selling flashlights. It was a seller's market and he was getting twenty bucks for a five dollar flashlight that probably wouldn't last a week. "Only two left," he said.

Josh pushed aside his cheapskate persona long enough to part with a twenty, unable to remember whether or not Kelsey had taken the one from the apartment. He turned the flashlight on, making sure it worked. "At least it works."

Tracey gave him a playful poke on the arm. He added sarcastically, "I can use it as a weapon if we're attacked." It was intended to be funny, but somehow, it gave him pause.

They hurried back to the apartment. At least there was emergency lighting in the stairwell and halls. "I just had to rent on the fifteenth freakin' floor," he muttered as they slowly made their way up the stairwell to their floor. In good shape or not, fifteen flights of stairs were hell on Josh's legs. By the time they reached the top, his quads were burning.

The fact that they had an electric stove ruled out cooking anything. There was no way to make coffee, so that was out, too. Tracey rummaged through the cupboards. "There's nothing. Not a damned thing. Wait."

She pulled out a box of stale soda crackers.

"We have beer, anyway."

Except for the half-empty carton of milk and a six-pack, the refrigerator was empty.

He twisted open two bottles of beer, handing one to Tracey.

She divided the crackers, handing a portion to Josh.

"Ugh, stale," he said, cracker dust spewing as he tried to choke down a cracker.

Tracey found a candle and they sat on the sofa, their feet on the table, eating stale soda crackers and clinking their beer in a toast.

"Remy doesn't need electricity," she said, immediately regretting her words. She was able to put Remington and the story out of her mind, and it now came rushing back like a tidal surge in the Bay of Fundy.

"I couldn't do school," Josh finally admitted. He thought he should feel something, sadness, guilt, even perhaps elation. He felt dulled to the idea of school, of exercising his big brain any more than it was already stretched by the hat.

Tracey tried to care, but couldn't find it in her.

That's the way they sat into the night: in the dark, side-by-side, drinking beer and choking down the occasional stale cracker. Tracey started to sniffle, and then she started to really cry. It was a soft, almost gentle sound, but it carried a heavy weight of pain.

"I think we are in way over our heads. We need help, Josh. Who can we turn to?"

But Josh had no answer to her question. He used his big brain to analyze complex mathematical formulae, creating order out of chaos theory, but this problem was something so out of his range, he felt like he was trying to move forward while his feet were stuck to the ground with super glue.

Then, a glimmer of a thought crept into the back of his awareness. He teased it out into the open and just as he had it in his grasp, the lights came on. Every light in the apartment was on and it was like suddenly being thrust into a giant camera flash.

The TV blasted on, the volume turned to an ear-splitting level. The clock radio in the bedroom joined the din; a news reporter was telling everyone about the blackout.

Before he let go of the thought he grabbed Tracey. "I have an idea. Tell me what you think."

Josh was through with school; there was no way to make up his classes in time—it would require every waking moment of his attention to do it. They were both addicted to the story, drawn sitting in front of Remington and letting the fedora work its magic, if that was even the correct word for what was happening to them. No, it wasn't the right word. Magic is a benign word, something leaning toward enchantment. The fedora was more...*supernatural*, leaning toward *eerie*, *weird*, *strange*, *peculiar* and definitely *unnatural*.

They somehow had to deal with all of that and reclaim their own lives. But the question remained: *How?*

Josh said again, "I have a thought."

This time, Tracey was curious. "What?"

"This is killing us, trying to do it this way. You quit work and now I have given up on school." Josh paused, trying to pull all the threads in his mind together. "When I tried going to school, all I could think about was the story—you sitting at Remington and typing away."

"I know what you mean." She completely stunned Josh by reaching in a drawer and took out a pack of cigarettes. Calmly holding a flaring matching to the end of the cigarette, she ignored the glare directed her way.

"I didn't know you smoked," he said. "When...?"

She snubbed his question, inhaling and finally puffing out a large cloud of smoke. She did that out of the side of her mouth with the kind of disdain smokers have for the rest of the world.

"What's your idea?" she asked, pointedly ignoring his last question.

"Instead of trying to live a normal life, we embrace this story. We face it head on." His ideas suddenly seemed so clear. "We go around the clock, changing places, the way wrestlers do it. You know, what do they call it? 'Tag team.' We tag team. You write as long as you can. When you are too tired to go on, you let me know and I pick it up. I go as long as I can until I have to stop. We keep that up until this damned story is finished and sent off to NANOWRIMO."

"It might work," Tracey said, finally snubbing out the smoke in an improvised ashtray—an empty can that used to contain tuna fish.

Tracey wished she could walk back to the studio so she could lovingly caress Remington, her hand draping over the cool metal of the typewriter cover. When she talked about it, it was oddly sexual, and Josh felt a growing erection. *That will have to wait,* he thought, pushing the feeling aside to concentrate on their plan.

"You have been at it all day. You need your rest if we are really going to do this. There's an old mattress leaning against a trash bin. I saw it on our way here, about a block away from the studio."

They locked up the apartment and walked back to the studio, stopping to look at the mattress along the way.

Tracey wrinkled up her nose as she inspected it. "I guess if you ignore the stains it might work." She sniffed it closely and shivered a bit. "At least it doesn't stink, too much."

They struggled it back to the studio and dumped it in a corner of the room. It wasn't long before Tracey was asleep, mouth agape, snoring loudly.

Josh sat in front of Remington and put the ear buds in and powered on his MP3 player. It wasn't enough to cover the sound of her guttural snoring, but it certainly helped. That woman snored like a man.

He put on the fedora, thought briefly of Humphrey Bogart, and began. This time, they were going to tag team and take the story through to the end.

chapter

THIRTY
NINE

After two days, Star determined Fortuity was strong enough to walk once again. "We are almost there, but we can't delay any longer," he told the rest.

Searcher helped the newcomer to her feet and she nodded that she was ready. A gentle wind blew in from the south, promising a warm day, not too hot, and perfect for walking. They walked until the high sun was overheard and sought shade, spreading their belongings and lazing under the graceful limbs of a large oak tree.

"Star?" the question came from Searcher.

Star anticipated the question. "I know. We have too much to carry. My mother told me about the desert people. They carried little and existed from day to day." He looked at all they were trying to carry. "We live in villages here, relying on our needs to be stored. We never worry about moving from place to place."

Blossom was lying on her side, listening.

"Are we becoming nomads, destined to wander?"

Star knew they were uncomfortable leaving the safety of village life. He appreciated the sacrifice they made to follow him into unknown territory, unknown lives. But he also knew from his mother that there could be a new life lived by other people and the animals that lived around them.

He observed an abundance of game as they walked. He had seen deer, rabbits, game birds, and other animals that would sustain them. He saw plants growing—the kind he knew to be edible. Some plants carried seeds that could be stored and later used to cultivate the plants without having to forage.

"Look," Searcher shouted and pointed.

A small horse grazed just beyond the small hill to the east. Searcher stood up and started walking slowly towards the animal. He was a man accustomed to the nature of animals and knew how to approach the wild horses without alarming them.

The horse stopped its grazing and looked up at Searcher in curiosity. It was a grey color with white mottled spots. A dark grey mane rippled in the light breeze as it continued to chew the mouthful of grass. Dark brown eyes changed from curious to caution as Star drew closer, but the horse didn't bolt. With a snort, the horse shook its head and pawed at the ground with its right front foot, backing away slightly.

Searcher talked in low, calming tones and continued his approach. He was close enough to reach out and touch the animal but didn't. He kept the monotone words in play, watching the horse relax. Searcher reached slowly into the folds of his wrap and pulled out an apple. He was saving it for his own nourishment but now offered it to the horse instead. After a short pause, the horse turned and accepted the apple, crunching and chewing through stem and seeds.

With a practiced move, Searcher gently reached a hand and placed his fist over the mane. Star, Blossom and Fortuity watched in fascination. The horse responded well to the touch, accepting the authority in Searcher's firm hand, knowing if this man could feed him, he also would take care of him.

Searcher turned and called out softly to Blossom, "There is a tether in one of my bags. Bring it to me."

When she walked towards Searcher and the horse, the animal became wary, but his handler relaxed the beast with soothing words and soft strokes to his nose. Soon the horse was tethered and Searcher led the animal back to the shade of the tree. The horse almost resisted as he neared the others, but obediently followed under Searcher's firm guidance.

That singular event made it possible for the four of them to continue on as they had. Searcher was an expert at tying the load onto the back of the animal. That afternoon, they started walking again, freed from carrying their heavy burdens.

Blossom quit counting the days and nights. She noted instead the change in their surroundings. They long ago left the low country, with its lush green grasses, plants and trees. They skirted around many villages. Some of the villagers would wave and even offer food and water. Others were wary and simply watched their strange group pass by.

They walked higher into the hills and mountains. Blossom had been taught to be wary of the highlanders. The highland people looked different than she imagined, yet often acted friendly, offering food and drink as they passed through.

"I know a bit about them," Searcher said one day. "I met some when I was hunting not long ago."

"They are no different than us," Star said. "They are just trying to survive, the same as us. They will do what they need to do. They will protect themselves when they feel threatened. But, they know we mean them no harm."

Fortuity knew the truth in what Star was saying. But the memory of her kidnapping and rape was still too fresh in her mind for empathy. As time passed, it became obvious one of her captors was successful in his attempt to breed: she was with child. She was not in a forgiving mood and she refrained from contributing her thoughts on the subject.

They walked on, past the highland villages and over the low mountains. The trees thinned, the terrain stretching into grassy plains that went on for miles around. The first sight of a bison was astonishing to them all.

"Those magnificent animals are why we came to this place," Star said with reverence. "We will learn to take care of them, to take what we need for food, and their skins will yield many uses for us. Nothing will be wasted."

"What about grain?" Blossom asked, missing the wild oats that had grown around her village, the fields worked and harvested by the village men.

"Look," Star said, pointing to the heavy green stalks rising from the earth nearby, "That is a new kind of grain. It is maize. I have followed the words of the ancient elders to find the bison and the maize; they are our destiny."

That night, camped in the open, he told them about Stargazer. The night was warm, but there was a touch of the cold to come.

"My mother knew Stargazer. He was the man who read the stars and led her people, following the food and the animals whose hides provided clothing, protection from the elements."

Blossom heard rumors of such a story.

"Before he died, he showed her the secret paths of the stars, and she passed his knowledge and voice on to me."

The darkness enveloped them, and Star pointed to the heavens, the galaxies were strewn across the sky on this cloudless night.

"He told her to follow the drinking gourd," he told them, pointing to a particular constellation of stars in the sky. "There, do you see it?" Later peoples would call these same stars the Big Dipper.

He listened to their low sounds of murmuring; they saw and wondered as he explained the mysteries of the night sky.

"Stargazer gave my mother the secret to escape, to find a place of safety, and to give birth to me. Your people became my people," he said, looking directly at Blossom.

"Stargazer is there," he said, pointing out the outline of a face in the stars. "That is Stargazer, next to that bright star. "The bright one there is my namesake." Unbeknownst to Star, he was gazing upon the North Star. He didn't tell them about his sacred conversations with Stargazer, however; they would not understand the whispers of a dead man he often heard on the wind.

As Blossom and Searcher pondered this Fortuity suddenly let out a moan. "It is my time."

Blossom left the village before her coming-of-age ceremony, but she was a young woman with the knowledge needed from watching many of the births her mother, a midwife, attended. She solemnly ran the errands and brought the water. Every birthing was different. Some lasted for days and some started and ended before a full journey of the sun. Some, unfortunately, ended with either mother or child returning to the earth. For Fortuity, the labor was hard and painful, but exceedingly quick. Soon, she was holding a new baby, laying it on Fortuity's chest as she worked on the cord and afterbirth. It was an ancient custom. She threaded a long fish spine with dried tendon and stitched the torn flesh while Fortuity was still exhausted and excited, numbing her to the pain of the stitches.

She turned to cleaning the babe with warm water and a cloth, swaddling him in a blanket when he was clean. She smiled at Fortuity, who nodded her head in approval.

Blossom cradled the child in the crook of her arm and parted the blanket covering the lean-to they built to shelter the sacred labor from male eyes. She crawled out and walked around the fire to the edge of the small make-shift camp, presenting the new child to the men who waited.

Star looked down at the still squalling child and said to Searcher, "This is our sign. We will begin building our new village. This is where we will stay. Our wandering is over."

Star and Searcher worked tirelessly and Blossom was no stranger to heavy lifting and construction. Fortuity took over preparing and serving food, rendering animal skins and other lighter work while she mended and tended her child.

Searcher wanted to ask Star where he learned how to make the bricks. The villages they knew consisted of huts made of thatched grasses and tree branches. They were protection from the elements, but did not stand up to strong winds and certainly did not stand up to fire. Fire was a constant concern in the old village. But he knew that Star held the source of his knowledge very close, and most of the time Searcher did not wish to know. Something in Star's eyes spoke of mysteries too eerie to be revealed. There was something of the ancient dead in that man's eyes.

But Star taught them how to mix the right mud with sand and water, pouring the mixture into forms and letting them bake in the sun until they became sturdy blocks for building. He showed them a stream that had a special mud, mud that would bind the block without crumbling or cracking. Soon, they constructed a village of four huts. One was for Star. Blossom claimed one as a center of hospitality and warmth. She decorated it with flowers and other adornments.

Searcher thought he would surprise them when he announced his intentions to live with Fortuity and become the father of the growing boy. But Star and Blossom recognized his intentions long before he did. They looked at each other and smiled when Searcher made his announcement. Searcher and Fortuity made their home in one of the huts and were soon settled in comfort.

The fourth hut was designated for storage. It was a place to keep food, provisions and skins.

At first, Star was puzzled by trying to find a way to make the roofing more permanent and sturdy. He experimented with large limbs dragged into camp from the nearest woods, notching them with a stone axe to fit over a long central beam. He filled the gaps with mud and embedded long grasses and straw as the thick mud baked dry.

A large enclosure soon contained seven horses. They built it near the village, against a small outcropping of stone. It had taken Star some time to learn how to make the holes in the posts without splitting all the way through the wood. Searcher felt good finally being able to teach the young buck a thing or two. Searcher was an excellent horseman and the others served as his workers. They used the horses to drag the larger limbs to the village. It wasn't long before the two men were adept at lifting them to the top of the adobe bricks. The roofing was susceptible to fire, they knew, but if a roof burned or was destroyed, the rest of the hut would still remain intact.

One night, they all roused to the sound of horses neighing wildly. "Something is wrong," Searcher shouted over the noise. He started running toward the corral and stopped in alarm. A pack of wolves brought down two of the horses and were savaging them. Some of the wolves were trotting off with large pieces of horse flesh in their teeth.

Searcher looked on, helpless to do anything to save them. In the morning light, they counted two horses killed and two that were seriously injured.

"This is serious. I hate those killers," Searcher spat out the words in disgust, wringing his hands as though a wolf's neck lay in his grasp.

"They are only after food to survive, just like us," Star said, calming the other man. Searcher decided to build a small hut out by the corral with its own small fire pit, allowing him to keep watch during the night should the beasts decide to return. The two maimed horses were beyond his help and he did what needed to be done and put them down. The others noted the tears in his eyes and knew how hard it was for him to destroy the living things. Though they dried the horse meat, it had a tangy flavor that wasn't popular among the group. They never tried to eat horse flesh again.

One day, a man and woman arrived, walking over the crest of the nearby hill. They called out their arrival to the four, who paused in their chores to watch the couple approach. The man held up his arms in a gesture of good will. The woman carried a baby in a papoose. They looked weary, but otherwise in good spirits and health.

The man looked at Star and said, "You are The One we have searched for." It wasn't a question. Star smiled and clasped the newcomer's shoulder in welcome.

The man proved to be a hard worker and they soon added a new hut to the village for the family. It was comforting to see the children together. It was a sign that their tiny village had a future, as each person accepted their season, knowing life ended and the youngsters would carry their stories with them and pass them on.

As time passed, Star and Searcher hollowed out a large log to hold water in a trough. Though a tiny stream wound its way through the plain not far from their village, walking down and filling a bucket several times a day seemed a waste of time. The trough worked especially well during the rains, when it would fill up on its own, creating less work for the inhabitants.

One day, it was some time later, Star was standing at the water looking at his reflection when he realized enough time passed that he was now entering his middle years.

He looked around. Fortuity's child and the others had seen a number of seasons and were enjoying the last years of their playtime. He knew they would all-too-soon be expected to take up the yoke of responsibility and secure their place in the village as adults.

Let them enjoy the play while the time is still there.

The village was growing. One-by-one and in couples, the others came. One time, an entire family of father, mothers and four children arrived together shortly after the winter melted away. The entire village helped them build their own hut, large enough to house all six of them.

The village now took on a comfortable look. Trees had been planted during their first year at the site and were now taking shape, providing esthetic as well as practical results. Gradually, they built a low wall around the entire perimeter. Star anticipated a growing population and designed the wall to accommodate expansion. The wall snaked in a zig-zag fashion around the settlement.

Smoke rose from small cooking fires as well as the large, central fire pit. The sounds of work filled the air as women cooked and prepared animal skins and other such tasks imperative to the survival of the village. Men came into the village carrying grain and other food stuffs on large stretchers from the fields nearby. Other men rode in on horses, proudly holding up game they caught, game that would be used for food and clothing. This period of the village's life was called "the happy time," and Star felt he was finally fulfilling his destiny that was written in the stars.

He still walked out into the countryside to commune with Stargazer. His visits, however, became less frequent as time went on, and he felt less inclined to talk to the old man in the stars.

Star's complacency was shattered during one of his rare visits alone in the open night sky when he sensed something in the whispery words from the stars. His mother was dead, they told him. He didn't know if he truly heard the words or simply absorbed the information from the earth itself. He was filled with profound grief, though he had not seen her in the many years that passed since he left his home. He never told the others about the news, but they felt his sorrow for many weeks thereafter. When he finally came out of his mourning, he called a meeting of the people. Soon the village was organized. A group of elders, men and women, were selected to make important decisions for the village as a whole, to serve as a council of wise ones to guide the people when Star's time to return to the earth would inevitably come.

"We need rules to lead us," he told them, and he asked the elders to formulate laws they could all live by. His intention had been to create a set of simple, benign laws they could all accept that would improve their lives and guide their people when he was no more. He was not prepared for what followed. Everyone had their own idea of what the rules should be. Soon, the list of potential rules and laws was extensive.

One man stepped forward and claimed the right to sit in judgment when disputes broke out over interpretation of the new laws or when one was violated. His offer was accepted by the elders with some reluctance, though the man was of an age to claim the role by right of experience. Soon he appointed a large young man to police the village, enforcing the decisions made by the judge. Star watched these happenings and felt uneasy. This was clearly not his intention.

Star had better luck establishing a school, however. Soon they had a place where knowledge could be organized and shared. This led to a rapid increase in communication and language in the village. The woman who headed the school was the most admired person in the village other than Star: It was Blossom, and she knew then why she followed him on an unknown journey on that day so long ago. The children were drawn to her and she responded with unconditional love. Her long-suffering patience helped, too.

Star slipped into a period of vanity. He began to believe he created a new paradise where all could come to live in harmony, to be as one. The weather was close to ideal. The people drawn to the settlement were the right people. There was ample food and game. They were now organized in defense of wild animals, even making offerings of food to the marauding wolf packs during the winter time.

All because of me, Star thought to himself. *I have fulfilled Stargazer's prophecy, my mother is dead, and a strange and hostile world is far away on the other side of the harsh, high mountains.*

One night, he looked up at the stars, ignoring a pleading voice whispering on the wind. He felt he no longer needed Stargazer's wisdom or lessons; he accomplished his mission and was satisfied to live out his days in happiness and plenty. He turned his back on the night sky and went into his hut to sleep.

The following morning, he looked to the far south, some inner turmoil forming in his breast. Storm clouds covered the mountain tops. Suddenly, for just a moment, the clouds parted to reveal a pass between them. He didn't realized the significance of that place—the pass through which his mother fled to carry her unborn child to safety.

As he prepared to turn away, he saw a flash from the point where the pass led between the mountains. He paused, unsure of what it might be, but he pushed away the small stream of fear that trickled into his heart at the sight and turned away. When he looked back over his shoulder, the storm clouds once again obscured the mountain pass. *It was only my imagination,* he tried to tell himself, but suspected that it wasn't.

chapter

FORTY

Weeks passed into months, and months turned into years. Years passed with the settlement growing ever larger each season. The growing population brought with it the complexities of supply and demand, the differences in philosophies and experiences of different peoples. More people meant more food was needed. Eventually, the settlement reached a point where specialization was required. Groups of workers formed in response to need. Builders were specialists in construction. They needed the expertise of the brick builders, who spent their days mastering the art of adobe.

Blossom watched her school grow and more teachers came to help. There was even a group of teachers and students who were doing primitive research, experimenting with ways to grow crops faster, with higher yields.

As the language of the tribe evolved, communication grew more complex. They generated symbols to represent words and ideas. They wrote them in the dirt and painted them with mud. They used natural dyes to paint their pots and animal skins.

When the settlement started to reach the limit of population it could support, Star called for a meeting of the elders.

"We need to find a way to send people out, to find new locations, to establish other settlements." Heads nodded in agreement and many chins were pulled, signs of sober thinking and great ponderings. Men and women with the requisite talents were recruited and trained to locate and establish their own settlement. After time, satellite villages and settlements sprouted up near the mother village, each at varying degrees of self-support.

Well-worn trails began to form lines of communication between the villages and settlements. Trading teams were established to travel into the low lands and highlands above the plains, and soon there was an active trading pattern with the other peoples of the outlying places.

At first, the highlanders and the low village people were delighted at the opportunity. But soon enough, the grumbling began, when they were required to meet trading demands at the expense of their own needs.

"Why are we sending away all of our good meat for trade when our people are going hungry?"

Such sentiment was becoming more and more common. The Uplanders, as they were called, of Star's village demanded food and animal skins in exchange for items that other tribes considered luxuries—items that did not provide nourishment or shelter from the elements. The imbalance in the trade was keenly felt by the villagers in the lower country and the seeds of rebellion blossomed.

Star mounted a personal mission to visit and placate the villagers below. He was still held in high regard, but his words were beginning to ring hollow and did little to ease the pangs of hunger in the other settlements.

The self-appointed Judge devised a network of law enforcers who began sending information back to him, telling him of the growing unrest. Unknown to Star, the Judge sent agents into the lower villages, men disguised as friends but whose business was to spy and report back any dissent serious enough to threaten the safety of the upland settlements. Some of the agents were a little too zealous in their mission to secure information and began to intimidate people for information.

The low-country villagers watched in horror as neighbor turned on neighbor and the enforcers went into the hut of one family who had been taken away, removing all the belongings and giving it to the turncoat who betrayed him. In this way, people were encouraged to make reports—even false ones—against neighbors they had known all their lives.

A small group of villagers held a secret meeting and the seeds of discontent grew. That sentiment spread through the lower villages like a wildfire.

Star rode out to the low country trying to make peace and was greeted with open hostility. He was shaken by the outpouring of discontent. In one village, a group of young men were emboldened enough to throw rocks at his passing entourage. He hurried back to his own settlement with alarm and called an emergency meeting to report his findings.

"There is only one response," the Judge told them. "We must form an army and prepare to defend ourselves. We need to go into the low country and take what is rightfully ours, to remind these ungrateful villages who they are."

Star listened but didn't say anything.

Others tried to reason a different approach. The female elders were led by Blossom and counseled talking and trying to understand what needed to be changed to make trade between the villages work again. As they tried to talk sense into the men, they heard an alarm shouted out.

"We are being attacked!"

Star and the elders climbed a ladder to the highest roof and saw a huge cloud of dust rising, nearing their village at an alarming pace. Through the dust they saw hundreds of men and women marching towards them with firm steps, waving weapons and shouting. It was terrifying.

Star ordered the gates closed, and after much yelling and posturing, the army of discontents on the outside finally started to drift away, satisfied they made their demands for fair treatment known.

The Judge stood by Star. He turned to those standing below and said, "Who now counsels peace? It is plain now—we need an army or we will be killed in our sleep at night!"

There were too many cries of support. In the name of self–defense, they shouted for an army.

Star had tears in his eyes and to his dismay, realized the matter was out of his hands. That night, he snuck out through the side gate and walked until he was away from the settlement lights. He walked until he could see the night sky clearly. He was much older now, and it was not easy to walk as he had in his youth. He tried to find a place to lay back and look at the sky. When he found a place and settled down, a terrible reality struck him. He could no longer recognize the patterns in the heavens. He could find no trace of Stargazer in the night sky. He didn't recognize his own star. He heard no voices on the wind. The memory of his mother was so faint now he could no longer remember what she looked like.

A comet shone like a flare and streaked across the sky. He watched the brief display flare into nothingness, returning the sky to dark. *I fear that is my star now, gone too soon.*

He was a desolate man when he returned to the village, his appetite gone and his bones aching. He walked the paths until he came to Blossom's hut. He raised his hand to knock when he heard voices. Pulling aside the deerskin hide covering the door just slightly, he could see Blossom and a circle of men and women squatting closely around a small fire. He heard her tell them that they needed to make preparations to leave their homes in stealth. No one noticed as he walked silently away, shoulders slumped in resignation.

Star never experienced such loneliness before. Blossom had been with him from the beginning, and now, she no longer had faith in him. The village he himself created, no longer listened to his counsel. They prepared to make war on people who were supposed to be their friends. He was a failure.

How can I abandon my destiny? What will these people do without me? He knew such questions were useless, more than useless, in fact. He walked the paths and heard the reality creeping in around him. The people of the village—his own people—succumbed to fear. They demanded an army to make them feel safe once again. They hardened their hearts against people of their own blood and demanded things that weren't their own, things they had not earned.

At the urging of the Judge, the energy and attention of the village shifted away from food and shelter. Their focus turned to weaponry. Groups of men busied themselves in the light of a bright fire. Star saw with horror that they were making spears. Another group to the side was fashioning clubs out of stout branches.

Their energy was not being channeled towards mere defense, either; these were weapons of offense, intent on killing. The stockpile of weapons grew at an alarming rate. Even the women were not immune: A group of women were busy amassing large quantities of food and cloth for wraps.

As he passed near the central fire, a cry went up, "All men to the meeting!"

Star stopped in his tracks, realizing he was not included in an important meeting. He followed the men to the clearing in front of the Judge's hut. Standing in the shadows, he heard the Judge speak.

"We must strike first. We will strike the highlanders villages first, with the swiftness of lightning in the summer. A group of you will be assigned to grab all you can carry and bring it back to the village to be shared. Anything of value must be taken." He paused for effect.

The crowd was pleased: they somehow felt entitled to the possessions of the highlanders, memories of a time long gone to justify the taking of things that were not their own. Everyone knew the story of Fortuity and what the highlanders had done to her. That story had recently been renewed and passed around at the command of the Judge, who smiled grimly.

When the murmuring died down, he held up his hand to silence the last whispers. "We must not be timid. We must kill the men and take the women."

Some shouts of resistance weakly spoke out.

Perhaps my people have not lost all sanity, Star thought. *Some, it seems must still have a small amount of honor left within their hearts.*

But the Judge held firm and his enforcers stepped forward with stony faces to support his decision. "We must kill the men who would kill us first! Take the child-bearing women and kill the rest. We do them no favors by allowing them to live to suffer starvation and humiliation. Remember, they share no such sentiments for other peoples during their times of need. They raided and killed and raped in the past. They deserve no pity and they deserve no quarter."

A collective gasp went out as each man realized what he was being asked—no, *ordered*—to do.

"What about the children?" someone in the back of the crowd asked.

"No male child shall be left. They will only grow to take revenge. We must be unbendable. We must make an example for the other villages. We will not be threatened. We will not allow other villages to rise up and tell us what to do."

"When?" someone shouted.

One of the aides raised a spear and shouted back, "Tomorrow we arm. Tomorrow night we rest. The next day, in the early light of the sun, we will begin. We will prevail. It is our right. It is our destiny!"

Star was reeling with emotion as he walked back to his hut. He knew that there were times when decisive aggression was needed. He thought back to the night he killed the men who abducted and raped Fortuity. *So long ago,* he shuddered at the passing of so much time.

This was different. This wasn't necessary, unavoidable violence. This was naked greed and evil. It *had* to be stopped.

But how?

He looked up; the stars were hidden from sight by the ambient light of the firelight from the settlement. No answers came from the night sky. It was a time to act, even if he was too old, even if it would be his last act of life.

He jumped up, sure of his evolving plan. He made no preparations, knowing there was little, if any, time for such a luxury. He didn't bother with food, either. His mind settled on a course and he simply acted. He crept to the stables and found his horse, the fastest of the bunch.

The horse quivered to his touch, picking up his excitement and ready for a long ride despite the hour. He put a blanket over the horse and swung his leg up and over with a light jump. Silently, he guided the horse into the shadows.

A young boy guarded the horses, but nodded to Star with respect and returned to his post. Star's late-night adventures were well known among the villagers. His actions never raised any suspicion, and tonight was no exception.

Star held the horse back to a walk until they were well out past the wall and passed into the dark of the night. When his eyes adjusted to the dark, he quickly located the trail he wanted. "Now," he whispered in the horse's ear and dug his heels into the sides of his horse. With a jump and a snicker from the horse, they raced into the night.

The clouds swept to the east and the bright light of the moon was all the horse needed to stay on course. At his rider's urging, the horse lowered his head and put on more speed, running like the wind.

From village to village, Star and his horse raised the alarm. He went from village to village throughout the night and soon the people gathered in the forest that ran along the foothills of the mountains, hidden from sight.

At midday next, the last of the stragglers wandered into the designated meeting space. Star led them to a clearing deeper in and laid out a strategy. Each man responded without question, and Star soon had each of them chopping limbs and trimming them into stakes. They knew they only had this one day and needed to make the most of it.

By the end of the day, the men were exhausted and fell to the ground in the clearing. The women circulated among the resting men with food and water and encouraging strength. Star saw the anxiety clearly on each face—man, woman and child.

After a brief rest, they planted the stakes in the field as planned, sharp side up and almost invisible. He then told the villagers it was time to leave and showed them the way deep into the forest and out the other side. Before they left, he made sure the raiders would know exactly where they entered the woods so they would race after them in their blood lust and greed.

He led the frightened group of villagers on into the night. In the early morning light, he could hear the cries of pain echoing in the distance and knew the raiders had fallen for the trap. Many of the men impaled upon the stakes would die horrible, painful deaths. Their pursuers did not follow the clear path they left out of fear of more traps, and the raid was soon called off. The Judge, sitting safely back on a hill, was livid. "There is only one person who could have organized this type of resistance. Star is a dead man."

chapter

FORTY ONE

The season changed and the Uplanders wasted their precious energy and resources on weapons in their vain attempt to take what they needed from the surrounding villages. It didn't take long for them to realize the consequences of their vanity and greed.

Unable to feed themselves, the old, the infirm, and the very young began dying first. Unable to keep up with the large numbers of dead, disease began to spread. A long rainy spell brought unnaturally cold weather in the spring and disease became rampant. Sick fathers and mothers recognized the finality of their existence and decided it would be more merciful for their children not to suffer. The unity of the village had fallen apart and every member lived only for themselves. No one would take in orphaned children, who would be left to starve. It was an awful choice, and often the parents took their own lives after killing their children.

Suicide was now becoming common, and homicide became ordinary, as the stronger men started to take away food and clothing from the weaker. Women began offering their bodies as a way to get food and stay alive. In this environment, the future no longer thrived.

It ended in a surprisingly short time. In human terms, the death of the village took years. But in the eyes of history, it was over as quickly as a blink of an eye. Over time, the wood rotted and the adobe huts and walls crumbled back to the earth, leaving no trace of the people who once lived, loved and thrived there.

The villagers in the low country lasted longer, but the disease drifted down with the mist and falling rain from the clouds. Coughing, fever, pneumonia and worse, swept through the peoples from highland to lowland.

In his waning years, Star wondered why he was still alive, why he was chosen for a destiny so bleak, to watch his ideas take root and flourish, only to die out in the end. It was almost more than he could bear. He was an old man now; he had nothing left in the world. The people of the lower villages always showed gratitude and respect for what he had done, but there was no one left to love him.

He was at his lowest point one day, sitting on a large rock in the middle of his new village, when he heard a familiar voice.

"Star?"

He turned, mouth open, to stare at Blossom. He was shocked, she aged greatly and now walked with a slight stoop, but he noticed her inner strength of heart as she came towards him. They embraced. It was something they had rarely done before.

"I never expected to see you, again," he said, amazed.

She put a finger to his lips to stop him, "Nor I you." She smiled, eyes wrinkling with true joy at seeing him.

They talked long into the night. The feeling of love rekindled between them brought them both to the same question.

Why had they not recognized the true nature of their relationship, what was actually between them before?

"I had a vision," Star began. "I couldn't sway-"

She put a hand on his shoulder to ease the guilt she knew was inside him. "I have always loved you Star, but I also knew my place. I served you always, as was meant to be. That was *my* destiny."

In the winter of their lives, they clung to each other.

"We have to leave this place," he said, shaking his head. "People are only going to die here. There is no future for any who stay."

"I know," she whispered and pulled his hand up to kiss his fingers. They held each other in an embrace that transcended love, each feeling bliss they never thought possible. They were still in each other arms when a voice came to him on the evening wind. The memory of the flash he saw not so long ago in the mountain pass in the harsh, high mountains to the south, came flooding back to him as they sat there. It finally made sense to him and he accepted what he needed to do.

With a firm hand, he touched Blossom on the shoulder, and once she was fully awake, he told her the plan. She smiled her approval and they walked back to his hut without any need for words.

The next day, they slipped away unnoticed by any of the villagers. There was nobody who really cared at that point. Two old people disappearing into the mists of the mountains made no difference among a people facing starvation, disease and death, even if one of them was Star.

They started walking in the cool morning air. This time, they headed south. As they climbed higher and higher, the wind blew pellets of ice and snow on their faces. As they reached even higher, it was cold enough that the snow gathered upon the ground without any warmth to melt it, and the snow made walking difficult. But Star and Blossom had both been born into a world that demanded toughness, and so they continued on undaunted, despite their age.

Soon they stood at the top of the mountain pass, looking back at the green vista below. It looked so warm and inviting, and they remembered the time when they were told by Blaze how she saw a similar view that held the promise of so much hope, but they both knew the reality hidden beneath the verdant fields.

Star knew this mountain pass. He knew it from the many times his mother told him about it. He smiled and told Blossom he could finally remember his mother again. She smiled up at him, remembering her own mother and that day so very long ago when they walked out of their family village without looking back. As the wind blew the storm clouds to the side, Star looked up into the growing light of dawn and saw the faint outline of Stargazer winking back at him once again. Star hoped it wasn't the last time.

He put his arm around Blossom and they started their walk down the desert side of the mountain.

"I can't go on," she said to him finally, easing herself down on a fallen log. Her shoulders slumped, and she turned her wrinkled face up at him, the weariness plain in her eyes.

Star tried to urge her on. "One step at a time, Blossom..." His words faded out, an almost electric crackling in the air.

"...trying...help...without me."

They both struggled for breath in the high altitude. They made another stop under a rocky ledge. It provided some protection against the wind following them down the mountain.

Star used some wood to...

Scratchy sounds and static disrupted the story, like a mistuned radio.

Then words came again to complete the sentence.

...make a small fire.

His supply was dwindling, he couldn't carry much. It was enough for now, however. They held their hands over the weak flame for warmth, and they pulled the bison skin around them and sat huddled, their words strangely interrupted by the same crackling, cackling static snapping in the air.

As fierce as the strong winds were, accompanied by the bitter cold, Blossom and Star gave thanks for their time together.

"How much farther do you think?"

Star wanted to give her a comforting answer, but he knew she wanted the truth.

"I don't know," he said—the truth in all its bluntness. "Mother only talked about the walk up this side. I don't even know how to find her people."

The next day, again there was static in their words, but neither seemed to notice.

A white, filmy haze covered the view.

When the words of the story cleared through the static, Star and Blossom were reaching a plateau where the snow stopped and the temperatures, while still cold, were at least bearable once again. Star told Blossom he had the feeling they passed the worst of their journey.

As Star stood looking out upon the desert, speaking to Blossom in soothing tones about their future, the static returned and a mist surrounded them as they stood there, unmoving. After a time, even the static faded until there was no more sound at all, only the enormous sound of silence.

chapter

FORTY TWO

Josh strained to hear those final words. Until now, the words for the story came to him and Tracey with ringing clarity. All he and Tracey needed to do was type fast enough to keep up. Now they heard a definite buzzing racket, as if the story were fading in a snowy blizzard. Then there was nothing, no more story, and total silence. Now, with the silence, he turned to Tracey in something approaching panic.

"I don't know what's wrong."

He took the fedora off; it was strangely cool to the touch now. When he put it back on, all he heard was a buzzing sound, and then that stopped. For some ridiculous reason, he thought shaking the fedora might help, sort of like hitting the side of an old-time radio, the kind with vacuum tubes, as though he could shake the words loose. It didn't help. He put the hat on and heard nothing but silence.

Tracey watched him, mutely wallowing in her own panic. Josh put his head in his hands, slipping his thumbs into his ears, trying to block out the sound of her breathing.

"Wait, I think I hear something." Josh's head tilted up, brow furrowed in desperate concentration.

Tracey looked at him, waiting.

"No, I can't make it out, something about rocks and sand."

"Are they out of the snow yet?"

"I have no idea." His eyes were wild and teary as he looked at her and shook his head, "I have no idea."

With resignation, he took the hat off and sat back. He looked as bad as he felt, exhausted and defeated. How were they going to finish the story?

He took the time to change the ribbon and polish Remy. He picked up the overturned pages of the manuscript and clacked them against the table to straighten them into neatness. A waiting pile of blank, new pages rested just beyond. All he could do now was to keep staring at them.

Josh leaned back and stretched, noticing just how tired he was. He put the hat back on and listened, his eyes closed. "Still nothing, he admitted." He took the hat off once more.

"Would you like coffee," Tracey asked, hopeful. It was all she could think of to say.

Josh took his coffee very seriously, and even in this state, he didn't trust her ability to make it right, even though she often did.

"You try," he said. He got up and made the chair available for her, passing her the fedora.

"I'll make the coffee, very strong, I think."

Tracey sat down and picked up the hat. Josh turned from his coffee making in expectation. He could tell from her posture that no words were coming to her, either.

"I don't know..."

He watched her shoulders start to shake, slowly at first, and then she wrapped her arms across her chest grabbing her shoulders with her hands. With that, she started to cry. It started as a soft weeping, barely audible. Soon, however she was shaking and wailing in loud, gasping gulps. Josh stopped in the middle of measuring out the coffee and came over to her.

He tried to comfort her, but she slapped his hands away.

"This is awful!" she howled.

Neither knew what to do, so they did absolutely nothing. Well, that isn't exactly true. They actually started what was to become a very memorable fight. Fighting was something they hadn't done up to now. They bickered or squabbled perhaps, maybe even robustly disagreed a time or two. But they never once crossed that line that turned a disagreement into an actual, honest-to-goodness *fight*.

This time it was different. It was like two addicts going through withdrawal under the same roof; they turned on each other like piranhas in a bloody feeding frenzy.

Recriminations began, each accusing the other for the current state of affairs. They both stormed around the studio, pointing their fingers and yelling. Tracey threw a half empty coffee mug at Josh. He ducked and the cup sailed over his shoulder and shattered against the wall behind him. It left a trail of tepid coffee in a comet-trail pattern in its wake. Josh looked down at the coffee stains on his shirt.

The recriminations increased, coming as fast as bullets spraying from an Uzi, blame ricocheting around the room, echoing the anger that began to approach positively hateful.

They paused long enough in their battle to try the fedora once again. Josh picked it up first. "There's no heat, it just feels like any other old hat." He noticed for the first time just how stained it was.

Tracey snatched it out of his hand. She turned it over and around, looking and feeling for any signs of the old warmth, any sign that it was something other than just an old, worn-out fedora. She threw it on the table, where the hat teetered for a moment before stopping, upside down, unceremoniously resting next to the manuscript.

She ripped the last page out of the typewriter platen and looked at the words. The last sentence was unfinished, just like the words, just like the story.

Whether it was the tension, the exhaustion from their tag-team effort over the past several days, or the fading of the words, the two of them both felt the fedora had abandoned them just when they needed it the most. The story, instead of ending with a bang or even a flutter, just faded away with no conclusion. It was like making love until just before climax, and then having someone throw ice water all over you. It was a thoroughly unsatisfying shock to the system.

Through it all, Remington sat silently during the rage, waiting with a style that only machines have, patient and ready to go on with its task, a task that unfortunately required human input. But both Josh and Tracey were exhausted. Not enough to stop the fighting, of course.

It evolved into a portable fight, one they moved around the studio. When that wasn't enough, they moved it into the hallway. They moved it to the freight elevator of the loft building. They moved it for blocks, and as they walked, passers-by stepped aside. No one wanted to intervene, to take sides, and no one even knew what they were really fighting about. Onlookers were puzzled by the heated shouting, something about a talking hat, as best they could gather. It made no sense to anyone listening to the two yelling at each other.

They finally moved the fight up the elevator until they were back in the apartment. The fight hadn't abated; indeed, it really picked up speed. Tracey carried the fedora and was threatening to rip it to shreds, although the threat was entirely hollow. Every time she tried to even rough it up a bit, something inside her prevented it.

She also carried the manuscript in the other hand and in the heat of one moment, threw pages against the wall so hard they scattered from one end of the living room to the other. She stomped, kicking at pages until the floor looked like it was covered with a fresh blanket of snow.

Josh lugged Remington back to the apartment under one arm and then the other, and welcomed the chance to put it on the kitchen table. It was heavy, and his arms were aching from the seven-block battle.

The decibel level of the fight ultimately decreased, but not the intensity of the accusations or threats. At one point, Josh picked up Remington and stormed out on the balcony, holding it over the railing, threatening to drop the typewriter from the fifteenth floor. He didn't, of course, but he did slam Remington down rather hard on the table without concern or apology.

The two stood toe to toe and glared at each other, neither one willing to give ground, to concede even one inch.

Then, like a tire suddenly deflating, they stopped in mid-recrimination. The silence was only broken by the banging on the wall, their neighbor pleading with them to stop yelling.

They didn't look at each other and offer reconciliation; they just stared. They each had the same blank stare. It was that look of a junkie, long past the need for a fix and helpless to go on.

Finally, they turned away from each other, not an ounce of compassion exchanged between them. They walked into the living room. Josh sat back on the sofa, which groaned displeasure at his flopping down. Tracey walked through into the bedroom but didn't close the door. She just dropped on the bed, a bed that remained unmade for weeks.

They didn't talk, but stayed in their respective places, like two boxers in the corners of a ring, waiting for the bell to signal the fight to resume.

There was no more neighborly banging on the wall and silence filled the apartment. If there actually was a mechanical clock anywhere in the place, they would have heard it ticking. All they heard was the persistent dripping of the kitchen faucet, the result of an old washer. Tracey even heard it from the bedroom.

Josh sat back on the sofa listening to the *plunk, plunk, kerplunk* of the faucet and slowly realized that he would never know the end of the story.

He looked in at Tracey and finally felt a pang of guilt. In his remorse, he stood up and walked into the bedroom.

Tracey, hearing his footsteps said, "Go away, Josh. Leave me alone."

But her tone didn't agree with the words she expressed.

Josh sat on the edge of the bed, looking for something, *anything*, to say.

"We have a problem."

They started talking. And they talked long into the night. They talked about what they had given up, their sacrifices to the story, to the fedora.

"I wish I had never gone into that store. I regret the day I found Remington," Josh said morosely.

"It wasn't Remington, Josh," she replied, "It was the hat. Kelsey was right about it. You said she never did like that hat..."

Josh nodded, knowing she, was right. "That still misses the fact we don't have an end to the story. No one is going to believe any of this."

"Graham might," Tracey said.

"Who's Graham?"

"My grandfather," she said. "He always believes me."

"I have a friend who is so gullible he will believe almost anything, but even Garth wouldn't swallow this story," Josh grumbled.

They both knew it wasn't so much the story, but the way it came to them. Who would accept the idea of a talking fedora that could channel a story from before the dawn of history?

Josh said it for both of them. "All the time and energy we put into this."

"For what," Tracey replied, "nothing!"

But it really wasn't for nothing. They both believed they were witness to a very important story. They met, and got to know, characters who were now real to them. "They *are* real," Tracey emphasized.

"And the events, I know those things really happened. I have to believe it, I just *have* to," Josh said, as if to convince himself.

"You did this for that novel in a month challenge," Tracey said. "Will you submit it?"

"I don't think so," Josh said quietly.

"Listen Tracey," he explained, seeing the heat growing again on her face, "I want you to consider something. If anyone finds out about this, they will have us committed. The shrinks will pull their chins, nod, and look up our diagnosis in the *Diagnostic and Statistical Manual of Mental Disorders*. Hell, they will probably find three or four new disorders to describe all this. Then one of them will write a whole paper on the "Fedora Syndrome."

Tracey nodded reluctantly.

Josh went on, "We need to make a solemn vow. We need to swear we will never tell a soul—*no one*. Do you agree?" Again, she nodded.

Once it was decided, they started to put their lives back in order. They started by ordering enough pizza to feed a crowd. Josh walked to the store for wine while Tracey started picking up the manuscript and sorting it back into its proper order.

When Josh returned with the wine, he uncorked the bottle and they sat with their legs across the table, next to the open box of pizza. After a few bites, Tracey got up and went into the medicine cabinet and came back with a razor blade. She knelt beside Josh and made a small cut in her finger and then one in his. They waited for a small drop of blood to appear and then mixed their blood together and swore an oath, "We promise to take this story, untold, to our graves. Pinky swear."

They started to laugh until they were both rolling over, kicking the pizza from the table, knocking over the empty wine bottles and scattering the manuscript pages. They relished the hysteria.

Mr. Remington and the fedora watched silently from the kitchen table.

Josh and Tracey were both hoping that life would return to normal. Tracey hadn't given thought to work or income since she being drawn into the hypnotic embrace of the story. Now, she cleaned the apartment and started to think about what she would do. She stared taking long walks for exercise and to think. She would buy a newspaper and walk to the coffee pub where she sipped coffee and got caught up on the news.

It doesn't look like I've missed much.

She read the classified advertisements, realizing how unqualified she was for most jobs. She ordered a refill and finished reading the paper. She turned past the financial and business news, never of much interest to her unless it was a story about some rich, good looking dude.

She was surprised at the sports news and events that happened while she was caught up the story. *At least the Steelers are almost in first place,* she thought as she finished the last of her coffee.

She enjoyed the walk back to the apartment, feeling the muscles in her legs flexing back into condition again. It was time to look for serious work. The one job she knew well would mean a lot of time on her feet.

Better that than working on my back, she thought with a chuckle.

Josh was a willing partner in getting the apartment back into a livable condition. He started paying attention to his grooming and surprised others with a slight change of wardrobe. He decided to shed the nerdy look. He even bought some new t-shirts at full retail, passing by his usual thrift shops.

The current academic term was a washout, but he impressed his advisor by sitting in on classes anyway and even starting some independent research.

"I will be ready to go balls to the wall when classes start next term." It was an expression he never used before, but a new Josh was finally emerging from a cocoon. *This* Josh even smiled and made small talk. In fact, he had a rather sexy smile when you took the time to notice. His old circle of friend even accepted him and welcomed him back with open arms.

He thought about this all as he rode his bicycle back from campus one day. He turned onto the bike trail, happy to avoid traffic, started to hum and then whistle. With his helmet securely strapped on, he was enjoying one of those days that was quite close to perfect. The temperature was cool, but the day was sunny and he rode with a smile.

He turned off the trail and found himself riding on the street where he found the store with the "Cheap Stuff" sign. He was no longer even curious. He convinced himself it was merely a hallucination, a figment of his imagination and it no longer mattered. Remington and the fedora were both stuffed into the bottom of the linen closet in the hallway.

How much later was it?

Josh wasn't exactly sure, but one day, he walked into a sports bar, his arm protectively on the arm of the woman with him as he as he led her through the door, thankful for her love, for the warmth of their time together. He stole a quick glance at her and smiled.

As they walked up to the bar, he stopped and almost turned back around. He looked at the familiar woman behind the bar, drawing draughts and turning, laughing, to slide them down to two men sitting at the bar. He didn't have to ask her name; he knew who she was.

"Thanks, Trace," one of the men said, clanging a coin into the tip jar.

"Gee, thanks, Mel. A big whopping quarter, eh?" Tracey turned to Josh and met his eyes, looking at the woman with him. Josh and Tracey silently and privately acknowledged their past together with a brief nod.

"Hey guys, welcome to The Bullpen. What'll you have? Do you need a menu?" A secret smile for Josh turned up at the corners of her mouth.

Josh held up his hand and two fingers, "Beer for starters." Very casual-like, he thought.

"Kelsey, you remember Tracey? It wasn't really a question. What do you say, do we want a menu?" he asked the woman at his side.

"Hell yes, I'm famished," Kelsey said, smiling up at him and tugging on his tie, smiling at the woman behind the bar.

☙❧

Thanks for being a reader. I hope you have as much fun reading it as I did in the writing of it.

Remington and the Mysterious Fedora was written in 13 days as a part of the challenge to complete a novel during the month of November in 2009. It was a challenge I never dreamed of meeting, let alone having it turn out a story that I am proud of. Will I take up the NANOWRIMO challenge again? Time will tell.

Until then, I hope you enjoyed reading the story and I would appreciate hearing from you. Visit my website at www.write-byme.ca and leave your comments.

Chuck Waldron
Kitchener, ON
Port St. Lucie, FL

Made in the USA
Charleston, SC
26 June 2011